Sam kissed her softly, hesitantly, half expecting her to react with anger

But Susie didn't pull away. Amazingly, her hands came up to hold him, tugging gently at his hips to bring him forward and bridge the gap between them.

She turned her face up to his. For a long moment, he stared down at her in the moonlight, and then gently, wondrously, he lowered his face and kissed her as he had wanted to kiss her.

And just like that his universe shifted, realigned, settled. It was as if some giant jumble of jigsaw pieces was falling gently into place.

His world had been out of kilter.

Now it had settled where it ought to be.

Dear Reader,

Right near where I live is Swan Island, joined to Australia's southern mainland by a rickety, one-lane bridge. I walk my dog under the bridge and think what if, what if… Off goes my imagination, the dog sighs and my story starts. Thus I give you one boat crashing into the bridge, the bridge consumed with flames, a gorgeous heroine stuck with a fabulous hero—who just happens to be the twin brother of the father of her twins. Put in a heap of medical drama, the island's wonderful, eccentric inhabitants and a sizzling plot…and it's a book that practically wrote itself.

Find a picture of Swan Island on the Internet at http://www.queenscliffgolfclub.com.au/. As you can see, the island is famous for its golf course—and now, of course, its romance.

Enjoy!

Marion Lennox

HIS ISLAND BRIDE
Marion Lennox

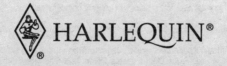

HARLEQUIN®

TORONTO • NEW YORK • LONDON
AMSTERDAM • PARIS • SYDNEY • HAMBURG
STOCKHOLM • ATHENS • TOKYO • MILAN • MADRID
PRAGUE • WARSAW • BUDAPEST • AUCKLAND

ISBN-13: 978-0-373-19918-1
ISBN-10:   0-373-19918-X

HIS ISLAND BRIDE

First North American Publication 2008

www.eHarlequin.com

Printed in U.S.A.

HIS ISLAND BRIDE

To all at Newington—your care keeps my butt in my chair writing the stories I love.

Special thanks to Susan, who made my introduction to Pilates a pleasure.

CHAPTER ONE

Dr Sam Renaldo's plans had never been detailed. He'd needed to leave—but he hadn't meant to burn his bridges in quite so spectacular a fashion.

The tiny town of Ocean Spray was on an island joined to the Southern Australian mainland by a single-lane bridge. Sam's plane had landed in Melbourne that morning and he'd driven straight to the island, thinking as he'd driven that this was a weird place for his brother's ex-girlfriend to live. It felt like the ends of the earth.

He drove onto the bridge, and it was almost enough to shake him out of the apathy that had been with him since his twin's death. The bridge was long and rickety, sea-worn timbers stretching across a tidal flat, with a wide, shallow river meandering through the centre.

He could hardly even see the water. The island was shrouded in fog.

There were some weirdly out-of-setting traffic lights at the start of the bridge. Technology in the middle of nowhere. The lights stayed red for five minutes, and he sat and waited and stared into fog as no car came from the opposite direction. Ocean Spray didn't look to be exactly a hub of tourist activity.

Finally the lights turned green. He steered his rental car out further onto the bridge timbers. The structure was more solid than he'd thought. It was OK.

The fog was thicker in the middle of the bridge. He could scarcely see.

And then…

He'd been concentrating on the bridge, not the river, and by the time he saw what was coming it was almost too late.

A massive boat, some sort of game-fishing cruiser, with three tiers of cabins, a satellite dish set on top and fishing rods everywhere, was lurching through the fog like a beast out of control. It was surging forward from the ocean, heading straight for the bridge.

Straight for him.

What the hell…

He shoved his foot on the accelerator and his car surged forward.

The boat slammed into the bridge behind him.

On the other side of the island Susan Mayne's pilates class was in full swing—or as much swing as was possible to achieve when the average age of her clients was over eighty. 'You need to pull that tummy in. Muriel, you'll never achieve core balance if you leave your tummy out.'

'I last tucked my tummy in when I was a bride,' Muriel said, trying mightily. 'I ate rabbit food for a month and I wore a whalebone corset. The night of my wedding my Harold took my corset off; he told me I looked prettier without it and my tummy's been free ever since.'

Susan chuckled. She knew Harold. Harold's beer belly matched Muriel's girth to a nicety. After sixty years of marriage Harold still thought his bride was perfect, and Muriel wasn't about to change now.

'You know I'm not interested in you changing shape,' she

told Muriel. 'But you are having back pain. That's why you're here. We need to get core stabilisation—your spine has to support all of you without your bottom or your tummy making you sway either way. So tuck that tummy in while you do your leg circles.'

'I'm trying,' Muriel gasped.

'Eh, Muriel, you look like I did when I was having our Eddy.' The lady on the trapeze—Doris—was giggling as she pushed herself through her own exercises. 'All strung up in stirrups ready to pop a baby.'

'Our Susan'd get a shock if a baby popped out, I'll be thinking,' Muriel retorted. 'When was the last time a baby was delivered on the island?'

'Too dratted long,' Doris said. 'There's so few young uns on the island. It's become a retirement home all by itself.'

'It's because of the bridge,' Muriel said wisely, sucking her tummy in with fierce concentration as she did wide leg circles with her weighted stirrups. 'If we got a new bridge with two lanes it'd make a world of difference. No one can depend on the bridge if they're commuting.'

It was true. Twenty minutes' drive away, on the other side of the bridge, was a railway line providing a fast train service to Melbourne. People lived on the mainland and commuted to the city, but with the bridge only having a single lane, when one broken-down car could block the bridge for hours, the number of people able to live here was severely limited.

'We're so lucky we have you,' Doris told Susan, and Susan grinned.

'You get those legs higher. Compliments will get you nowhere.'

'No, but we are,' Doris said, determined to have her say. She pushed her pelvis up with equal determination. 'You provide the only medical service for the whole island.'

'A pilates studio is hardly a medical service.'

'You do the emergency stuff as well,' Doris said stoutly. 'And your pilates clinic is a medical service. Before you came here I was a wreck. I was using my scooter to get around. You have me walking again.'

It was encouragement as much as anything, Susan thought as she adjusted the weights for Maggie's arm stretches. Left to herself, Doris had been miserable after the death of her husband, isolated by grief and pain and afraid to walk. Now, three times a week, Doris did her gentle pilates exercises, she had her fill of encouragement and companionship, and she was discovering life free from her scooter. She was one of Susan's success stories and she did her proud.

'Can we change the music?' Doris asked. 'If I'm going to swing here like a strung-up turkey, I need a bit of something fun. What about some of that hip hop?'

There were general groans, but Susan smiled and moved obligingly to the sound system.

And then she paused.

For the gentle piano concerto that had been playing had been replaced before she even reached the controls—by a crashing, splintering of timber, by a massive, ear-shattering explosion and by the sounds of disaster.

There was a hole where the bridge had been. Sam climbed from the car and stared in disbelief at the chaos behind him. The boat had cut a swathe through the sea-worn timbers. The rails on the far side of the bridge were still intact—by the time the boat had reached it its cabins had been destroyed, meaning the remainder of the boat had gone under, rather than through. He gazed in horror as what was left of the boat's hull emerged from the other side.

There was a man, still standing on the deck. The motor was still running. Hell, turn it off...

Too late. Like a roar from a cannon, the fuel caught and blazed, turning what was left of the boat into a fireball.

'Jump,' Sam screamed, but his words were lost against the fury of the flames. Sam had a momentary glimpse of a figure leaping for his life. Of a figure diving into the water, carrying the flames with him.

'The bridge is down.'

Muriel's yell followed her, for Susan was already outside, staring in horror at the bridge. She could hardly make out what had happened, but the glare through the thick fog was brilliant enough to tell its own story.

Muriel was right behind her, having freed herself from her stirrups in what must have been record time. Usually she waited patiently for Susan to free her, but not today.

'It's a boat,' Muriel whispered as the flames shot higher. 'Oh, God…Susan, run.'

Susan was already running.

Where the hell…

There. It was a fleeting glimpse, a figure against the flames. If Sam hadn't seen in which direction the man had jumped he could never have found him. But the figure from the boat was in the water, struggling, going down…

Flames were licking out toward him.

Sam couldn't go in there. The water under the bridge was covered in a sheet of flame. He ran further along the bridge toward the island, twenty yards to where the water was clear. No fuel here. Check again, he told himself. Suicide's no use to anyone.

He checked. The water under him was definitely clear. A school of minnows darted under the bridge timbers, illuminated by the sheets of brilliant light. If the fuel had reached here there'd be a sheen. No sheen. Go! Now.

He kicked off his shoes. He checked once more that he could see what he was aiming for. He jumped.

Susan was running. Halfway across the bridge, just before the smashed timbers, there was a car. Empty. Its driver's door was open.

Where was the driver?

The flames were licking up the timbers. Any minute now they'd reach the car.

Susan was desperately trying to get her shocked mind to think. This car was intact. It hadn't been the cause of the crash.

So a boat had smashed into the bridge and the driver of the car had…Had what?

A spurt of flame licked forward from underneath the car, signalling its own warning. She backed away, leaving the car to the flames.

Where? Where?

She was the only person on the bridge. Her pilates clients weren't fit enough to get here over the rough timbers. They'd be phoning for help, but for now there was only her.

Someone must have been on that boat, and someone had been in the car. If they weren't on what was left of the bridge then they had to be…in the water?

The fog was swirling into smoke, the flames a surreal glow. She was too high above the water. She couldn't see.

There were rails between the bridge's pylons. She swung over the top of the bridge railing and climbed down.

Where?

Where the hell…?

Sam surfaced just out of range of the fuel oozing out from the wrecked boat. Where…?

The fog and smoke swirled away a little, letting him see. A figure, struggling. A hand raised, in the middle of the slick.

The flames weren't here yet. There must have been one spurt of fuel and then another, as there were two slicks and only the one closest to the boat was alight. But they were drifting together already. Any minute now the flames would sweep across the surface of the water to reach the second slick. He had seconds.

Sam took a long, considered look, forcing himself to take time, judge distance.

He took one last, long breath and dived.

She could see someone backlit by flames, in the centre of an oil slick, and that slick was desperately close to the flames. He raised a hand, feebly, and she thought, Oh, God, she'd never…She'd never…

But then…

A figure surfaced beside the first. If she hadn't been transfixed she'd never have seen him. The newcomer surfaced, the first guy grabbed, the rescuer reached forward, breaking his lethal, clutching grip, swinging him round so he was facing away from him in a move Susan knew from lifesaving.

The fuel was igniting. It caught in one sweeping arc of flame. She screamed a warning, but the figures were gone, both of them, under the surface.

They couldn't have stayed under water for more than a minute but it was probably the longest minute of Susan's life.

She was under the level of the surface of the bridge now, balanced on a stay, leaning out, trying to see.

Please. She wasn't even aware that she was praying but she heard the words. Please.

No one.

And then the surface of the water erupted not ten yards from her. One head—no, two—one figure held firmly in the clasp of the other.

'Here,' she yelled urgently but they didn't respond. The smoke was blanketing them. They were free from the fuel slick now, but the slick was moving. She saw the flames licking closer.

There was no choice. She jumped into the water and struck out for them. Racing the flaming slick.

Please.

Where she'd come from Sam couldn't tell. His eyes were stinging, and he could hardly see. The guy in his hold was limp now. He'd struggled at first but then as Sam had hauled him underwater to avoid the oil, the guy had given one last wrench and had gone limp.

And Sam no longer knew where he was. The smoke was all around him, the flames reflected in the water, in the fog, so even knowing which way was up was problematic. He gasped for air, trying desperately to get his bearings.

And suddenly she was there. Right beside him. A woman, with blazing red hair swirling around her in the water, like the flames further out.

'Give him to me,' she gasped, and before he knew what she was about she'd slipped underwater, then surfaced against him, shoving herself upward between him and the man he was holding. She'd hauled the guy out of his grasp before he had room to argue.

'Follow me,' she yelled, and she kicked backward, then paused, waiting to see if he'd follow.

She didn't have to ask twice. He was coming. She swam like a fish, hardly slowed by the burden in her arms, or maybe it was because he was still gasping for air that she seemed fast in comparison.

But miraculously, gloriously, she seemed to know exactly

where the shore was. She knew where she was going and all he had to do was put his head down and follow.

There were shouts. 'Susan, Susan, Susan.'

And two minutes later he was in the shallows. People were surging forward, eager to help. Hands were grasping for him, half lifting him, hauling him onto the sandbank.

He was safe.

CHAPTER TWO

HE WAS no longer in control. He didn't have to be.

'Lie still,' someone ordered—a woman?—in a voice that seemed cracked with age.

'He'll have swallowed fuel. He'll be burned.'

'Susan's busy with the other one,' someone else said, sounding worried, as he took a couple of lungfuls of lovely clean air that was miraculously almost smoke-free. The breeze here must be blowing in from across the island.

'I'm fine,' he managed, wondering whether he was.

'Was there anyone else in the water?' someone else demanded.

Good question. Really important question. He tried to make his fuzzy mind think. That stretch underwater had been too long. It was taking him time to get his lungs in order. Blessedly, someone had fresh water. They were washing his face, pouring water over his eyes. He forced his eyes open, knowing he had to wash them, and finally things cleared.

'Not that I could see,' he managed at last. 'But I was in the car. I don't know who was in the boat.'

'We're checking now,' someone said, and whoever it was raised their voice and yelled to someone in the distance.

'Susan said check the water but stay well clear of any fuel slick. It can still burn.'

Susan, he thought, dazed. It was a Susan he'd come to find. Then he thought, No. How many Susans were in the world? It had to be coincidence. And now wasn't the time to be thinking of coincidences.

He was getting his bearings now, and his breath. There was a cluster of people around him. The girl—he recognised the hair—was working over a body. The guy he'd grabbed?

She was breathing for the guy, and pumping. CPR.

Hell.

The doctor part of him kicked in, hard and fast. He hadn't risked so much to let the guy die now.

'Let me,' he said curtly, shaking off restraining hands and moving swiftly to kneel by her side on the sand. 'Keep on breathing,' he said. 'I'll pump.'

'You can do CPR?' she gasped between breaths, not stopping.

'Yes.'

She had a mask fitted—someone must have produced basic first aid stuff. Breath, pump, pump, pump…She had the technique right, but doing effective CPR by yourself was an almost impossible ask.

'You breathe, I'll pump,' he said again, and she nodded, finishing the next round of pumping and moving upward to concentrate on getting air into the guy's lungs, leaving it to him to get the heart beating.

'Oxygen's coming,' she gasped, and went back to breathing as he started the pulmonary massage that might or might not save the guy's life. Probably not, he thought grimly. It had been tough enough on him, staying underwater so long, and he wasn't injured.

But miracles did happen. Thirty seconds later it seemed a miracle was just what they had. The guy's chest rose a little and then kept rising. A tremor ran through the guy's body and he jerked sideways.

The woman moved back fast, hauling the mask clear just in time for the man to retch violently. By the time he retched she'd already tugged him to the side, keeping his airways clear, so as he took a first choking lungful of air his airway was clear to let it in.

And then he took another. And another. They had their miracle. The CPR had worked. The guy was breathing on his own.

'Hey,' Sam said unsteadily, and sat back on his heels on the sand.

Now the lifesaving urgency was over, he had a chance to perform an overall assessment. He'd worked in ER in his training, and he'd seen patients come in like this. Trauma and burns were a savage mix and that's what they had here. The man must have been facing away from the full force of the blast, he thought. His face looked almost unscathed, yet the clothes on his back were a tattered, singed mess.

He'd been blasted into the water, Sam decided, or had jumped just as the thing had exploded, and the upside of that was that instead of being burned on his body, his clothes had protected him from the first savage heat, and immediate immersion had stopped the burning going further.

But his clothes hadn't protected him completely, and the blast itself had done some damage.

This was all figured out Sam's first sweeping glance, at the man lying prone on the sand, at the woman, the redhead, working over him competently, giving orders to the people around them, three or four very senior citizens…

'You've rung the services.' The woman hadn't relaxed yet. She was snapping out orders, looking grim. She was wearing some sort of gym outfit, he noted in that first assessment as he couldn't help but take in her appearance. Which was startling. She had on crimson leggings and a tiny white singlet top. Bare feet. She was soaking wet, as he was. She had seaweed hanging over her arm, tangling with her fiery red curls, which hung to her shoulders.

Her appearance right now was the last thing she was thinking about.

'Malcolm rang from the mainland,' one of the old ladies was telling her. 'With the bridge blocked it'll have to be the coastguard. Twenty minutes at least.'

'Damn,' Susan said. 'I need—'

'Bert's getting your gear for you,' the same old lady said before she could finish. 'We thought you'd need more than the first aid kit from pilates. He's backing your van down here.'

'Bert is?' the redhead queried, sounding scared. She whirled and faced Sam. She'd accepted his help without question while they'd needed to do CPR, and now it seemed like he was part of her assessment.

'Did you swallow fuel?' she demanded.

'No.'

'What about your eyes? Can you see?'

'They're fine.'

'Are you hurt in any way?'

'No,' he said curtly, 'and I'm a doctor.'

'A doctor.' Her gaze held. She'd been pale before but now every last vestige of colour drained from her face.

'Grant,' she whispered, and she sounded appalled.

'I'm Sam,' he said. This had happened to him so many times in his life that the response was automatic. He was a twin. Or…he had been a twin.

This, then, must be Grant's Susan.

But this was no time for the personal. 'I'm a doctor,' he said again, and she gulped and steadied.

'Right,' she said, obviously forcing herself to refocus. 'I…Great. But first…can you see the car backing down the boat ramp?'

'Yes,' he said. Two hundred yards away an ancient family wagon was weaving very slowly backward down a ramp leading from what looked like a public car park to the hard sand of the river bank.

'Bert's ninety-two and he has cataracts,' Susan said. 'I have a full emergency medical kit in the back of that car and I really need it to get here and not into the river. Can you help?'

She was holding her patient's head. The guy was still retching. He couldn't be left.

He was the doctor. Maybe he should…

'Don't fight it,' Susan was saying strongly to the guy on the sand. 'Your stomach's getting rid of a load of oil and that's a good thing. We've got you safe and the doctor's getting ready to give you pain relief. Dr Renaldo will be with you in a minute. As soon as he prevents another crash.'

She'd obviously prioritised and so should he. He went.

The next few minutes passed in a blur of medical necessity.

After that one incredulous gasp as she'd realised who he was—or who she'd thought he was—Susan had accepted with what seemed huge relief that he was a doctor, and she deferred to him absolutely.

It seemed there was no other doctor likely to be forthcoming. Only Susan, whatever she was.

She must be a nurse, and a good one, he thought as they worked together. The kit in the back of Susan's car was impressive, to say the least. Someone had brought towels, a vast pile of pink linen that they'd spread over the sand to give them the best possible workspace. The guy had roused to consciousness, then slipped away a little, moaning in pain.

But Susan's kit contained drugs, saline—everything he needed. Sam administered five milligrams of IV morphine, running fluids with an IV line, aware that the magnitude of these burns could be a killer. The guy's forearms and the backs of his legs seemed the worst, and adding to the complexity there was a vicious-looking wound on the back of his shoulder.

Sam worked on that, stemming the oozing blood, padding it firmly, aware that there'd be reconstructive surgery required further down the track.

'Is an ambulance coming?' he demanded.

'The ambulance might have a bit of trouble getting here,' Susan said ruefully. 'Someone seems to have knocked the bridge down. We'll wait on the coastguard.' Then: 'Hey,' she said, and she was no longer talking to him. Her patient's eyes had focused momentarily and she'd picked it.

'My name's Susan,' she said. 'What's yours?'

'H-Hammond,' the guy whispered. He was in his fifties, Sam guessed, a big man and florid. His clothes were ruined but he still had boat shoes on. Expensive.

As had been the boat. A million-dollar indulgence?

'Joe Hammond or Hammond Joe?' Susan asked, and Sam was astounded to see the man's lips twitch in what could almost be a responding smile.

'Pete Hammond,' he muttered.

'Hi, Pete.' Her hands were still working, spreading silver sulphadiazine on the guy's forearms, but she made it seem that all her attention was on her patient's words.

She was a mess, Sam thought. Her hair was littered with seaweed, her feet were bare and sand-coated...

She was smiling at her patient and Sam suddenly thought that if she smiled at him like that...

Whew. No wonder Grant had fallen for her.

'You've squashed your boat, good and proper,' she was saying, chatting easily to Pete in an 'over a cup of coffee' tone. 'Was there anyone else on board? Is there anyone else we ought to be looking for?' She asked it almost as if it didn't matter.

'N-no.'

'You were alone on the boat.'

'Yeah.'

Susan's shoulders slumped a little. As did Sam's. If there'd been anyone else in the cabin…Well, there was no way they'd have survived.

'Great,' Susan said, like it was no big deal. Moving on. 'But you've got a few burns and you've hurt your shoulder. No problem, but you're going to have to go to hospital and get things sorted. Dr Renaldo here has given you pain relief for the trip. It'll be kicking in any minute so hang on in there. We'll cover your burns, too—this stuff looks like food wrap—OK, it is food wrap—but it'll keep your burns clean. The coast guard will take you to Sandridge Hospital to do full assessment. Is there someone we can ring to tell them to fetch your pyjamas and a toothbrush?'

He had to hand it to her. Susan was reducing the situation to mundane and domestic with a few well-chosen words. Pyjamas and toothbrush. Pete closed his eyes but Sam was aware of the imperceptible relaxation, the slackening of muscles taut with the fight-or-flight reflex.

'Details are in my wallet,' Pete whispered.

His wallet was probably at the bottom of the river. Burned.

'You know, your wallet might be a bit soggy,' Susan said, still with a smile in her voice. 'Can you give us a name and a phone number we could ring?'

'Carly,' Pete whispered. 'My wife. We're staying in Seaspray Lodge in Sandridge.'

'Say no more,' Susan said solidly. 'Leave the rest to us. I have about fifteen interested onlookers here now and they're about to be relegated to phone duty.'

She did have interested onlookers. Horrified onlookers. They'd been arriving for the last few minutes and more were still coming. Sam was assisting Susan, lightly covering the burned areas in plastic cling wrap. It was methodical work, needing care but not complete attention, so he had time to take in his surroundings, the people around him.

His first impression had been that he'd ended up in some sort of geriatric facility. Now, though, the people around them included a few younger ones. There were a couple of burly men who looked like fishermen. There were two or three younger women, one with a baby. All were standing well back, not intrusive, just appalled, waiting to see if there was any way they could help.

'Donna,' Susan called, and the woman with the baby stepped forward.

'Yep.'

'I can depend on you not to sound scary,' Susan told her, and Sam saw a silent message pass—a warning. 'Can you ring a Carly Hammond over at Seaspray? Tell Carly her husband's had a fight with the bridge in his boat. Say he's a bit knocked about but it looks as if he'll be OK. Make sure she hears that, Donna. Tell her the coastguard's bringing him over to the hospital in about thirty minutes.'

She hesitated, then went on, 'When you ring, you'll get onto Faye at reception first. Tell Faye what's happening before you talk to Carly and ask her if she'll drive Carly to the hospital. Faye's a mother hen,' she explained to Pete. 'She'll make sure no one scares your wife.'

'I'm onto it,' Donna said, already moving away and calling back over her shoulder as she went. 'And I'll pick up the boys from school for you, Suse. Nick'll take them swimming and I'll give them dinner. Oh, and here comes the coastguard. Looks like the paramedics are on board. Too bad you've already saved him, guys, the hotshots are here.'

It was extraordinary, Sam thought.

Once the paramedics were there he could sit back and watch.

This was a tiny community. Everyone knew everyone. The chat was casual and friendly, everything seemed almost laid-back, but there was nothing laid-back in the way Pete was treated.

The paramedics worked with clinical efficiency behind their friendly banter. They seemed to know Susan well, and respect her. As they should, he thought. The first aid she'd offered had been stunning.

Why was she here? A soaked, seaweed-strewn woman in gym gear, amidst a host of elderly people on a tiny island at the ends of the earth…

At some time this woman had been involved with Grant. He didn't know how much, and now he was here he was even more confused. This was not the sort of place Grant would visit. And Susan…she didn't look like the sort of woman Grant would be attracted to either.

Mind, she was seen at a disadvantage right now. As he was. He was soaked, and now the urgency had gone out of the situation he was starting to shiver. Reaction?

He barely had time to think the word, and Susan was there, beside him. He'd retreated to a driftwood log half-buried in the sand, content to stay seated at a distance now the cavalry had arrived. The paramedics were loading Pete onto a stretcher to carry him the short distance to the boat. The onlookers were starting to disperse. Which meant that Susan could turn her attention to him.

Susan knelt in the sand before him and before he knew what she was about she'd taken his hands. Whatever shock she'd shown on first seeing him had been suppressed, and she was now all health professional.

She was gorgeous, he thought, dazed. A battered, sodden sea maiden.

'They're taking Pete across to the hospital,' she said, gently but firmly, hauling him back to the practical. 'I think you should go, too.'

'There's no need.'

'You're shivering. You dived under the fuel slick. Are you sure you weren't burned?'

'No. I didn't swallow or breathe in fuel and I got him out before the flames reached us. His burns were from the blast.'

'And your lungs?' She was still holding his hands, and it felt…strange. Weird. This was Grant's woman, he thought, or once she had been. What had happened between them? More and more he thought that this situation wasn't Grant's style. But Susan herself…No, she wasn't the sophisticated creature Grant had usually had by his side, but he could surely see why Grant had been attracted to her.

This was dumb. He needed to focus on common-sense stuff rather than how gorgeous his brother's ex-girlfriend was.

'My lungs are fine,' he managed.

'Let me listen to your breathing.'

'I'm OK.'

'Let me listen,' she said, more forcibly this time. 'Or I'll tell the coastguard guys to hold you down while I do. Doctors,' she said disparagingly, but she softened her words with a smile. 'They make the worst patients. You went under the oil slick and you surfaced in the middle of it. If there's muck in your lungs you know very well it has to be cleared or you'll end up with massive infection. The boat's going in two minutes so I don't have much time to decide whether to put you in it forcibly. So let me listen.'

'Fine,' he said weakly, and her smile deepened and she squeezed his hand.

'Good boy.'

'Hey, I'm not—'

'Shut up and let me listen,' she told him, and he did, which left him time to think about her, about how she'd dived into the water with no more hesitation than he'd had, and how she'd saved the guy's life, for if she hadn't appeared and helped drag him to shore the CPR would have been too late.

Grant might just have had solid reasons for getting involved with her, he thought. But more and more he thought she wasn't Grant's style. She was practical and sensible and...lovely.

She had a stethoscope to her ears. She hauled up his sodden shirt and listened.

'Cough,' she said, and he did.

'And again?'

Another cough. He was feeling more and more surreal. One minute he'd been driving along minding his own business, wondering who this Susan was, the next he'd almost died, he'd found Grant's Susan and now she had him half-undressed.

She was listening to his heartbeat. Listening to his lungs.

'I'm fine,' he told her. 'You jumped into the water, too. Did someone listen to your chest?'

'I didn't go anywhere near the fuel spill.' She sat back on her heels, a furrow of uncertainty etched between her eyes. 'Look, your car's destroyed. The bridge will be impassable. You'd better go with the coastguard.'

'I came to see you,' he said gently, and she flinched.

'Yes,' she whispered. 'I figured that. But there's not a lot to say. And I don't want you trapped here.'

'Grant died three months ago.'

She hadn't known. He could see it in the way she flinched, stilled, schooling her expression to be passive.

'Your...your brother?'

'Grant was my twin, yes. How long since you've seen him?'

'Eight years,' she said, taking a deep breath and looking back to the stretcher, to Pete, to things that were obviously her concern. As opposed to him. A reminder of an affair almost forgotten?

She'd remembered him. Or she'd remembered Grant. The shock when she'd seen his face had been real and deep.

'Look, go,' she said, sounding urgent. 'There's nothing for you here. I'm sorry about Grant but I'm really busy. If you want to talk to me then I'll get one of the fishermen to take me across for a couple of hours tomorrow. Leave me your number and I'll call you.'

He could do that. He could leave now, stay overnight at Sandridge, dry out the cheque that was currently soaking in his wallet in his trouser pocket and give it to her over coffee.

End of story.

That was what she wanted.

She rose, brushing sand from the seat of her leggings. 'I'm sorry, I have to move on.' The paramedics had Pete ready to move, and were clearly waiting for her to make a decision. 'This man will be coming with you,' she said.

'There are decent medical facilities in Sandridge?' he asked, and Susan obviously thought he was seeing sense. Her face cleared. 'There are,' she said. 'We have an orthopaedic surgeon and there's a plastic surgeon on call from the next town.'

'So Pete will be well looked after?' he asked, and the paramedic at the head of the stretcher nodded.

'Yes,' he said curtly. 'But we need to go.'

'Don't let me stop you,' Sam said, and he gazed around at the small group of onlookers still left. 'The information office at Sandridge told me that there's a bed-and-breakfast establishment here. I have a tentative booking at Mrs Murphy's.'

'Ooh, that's me,' Doris said, and the old lady beamed her delight. She'd obviously been horrified by what had happened but was now aching to be included. 'I'll take you home right now,' she said. 'And don't you worry about petrol in his lungs,' she said to Susan. 'The moment he starts coughing I'll ring you straight away.'

'He should be under observation,' Susan said, but she was fighting a losing battle. The paramedics were already moving Pete toward the boat. The morphine Sam had administered was taking effect—Pete looked up at them sleepily and gave a shaky wave of farewell.

'Thanks,' he croaked, and Susan smiled and slipped back to his side.

'You take care,' she said. 'We'll get the local fishermen here to look after what's left of your boat. Don't you worry about a thing—just get better.'

He hadn't spared a thought for the boat, Sam thought, startled. What the hell was Susan about saying she'd take care of it?

But then…It had been an expensive cruiser, set up for serious deep-sea fishing. It'd be worth a fortune and it'd probably be this guy's pride and joy.

He might not be voicing concern about it but it'd surface over the next few hours, when Pete was in a situation where no one could reassure him.

Susan had pre-empted that. As a medic she was seriously good.

Even though she'd appreciated his help, in a medical sense she probably could have coped without him.

'I wouldn't have got him out of the water in time,' she said as they watched the paramedics carry Pete to the coastguard boat tied up at the jetty.

He was startled. Were his thoughts that obvious?

'It's not too late to change your mind,' she said obliquely. 'The forecast is for the wind to get up. You might be stuck here for a couple of days.'

'That's OK,' he said. 'It's going to be a red-tape nightmare replacing my hire car, and I need to talk to you anyway.'

'I don't think you do,' she said, hugging herself, and he thought suddenly she was as cold as he was. The wind off the water was brisk. They both needed to get dry and warm.

'It can wait until tomorrow,' he said.

'It can wait for eternity as far as I'm concerned,' she said bluntly. 'I'm really sorry to hear that your brother is dead, but Grant decided not to talk to me almost eight years ago. I'm not interested in resuming the conversation with his twin now.'

There was no more conversation forthcoming with Susan. She disappeared to get dry and Doris took Sam home.

Doris's bed-and-breakfast establishment was the old light-house keeper's residence on the far side of the island, set high on a bluff looking out to sea. From outside it looked stark and weather-beaten, an ancient stone cottage with walls that looked more like a fortress than a residence.

It looked great from the outside, but then he walked inside and discovered it was just about the last word in kitsch. Doris had decided on a marine theme and had gone overboard. Her lights were sea lanterns. There were craypots dangling from the ceilings and fishing nets strung between. She had ships' wheels on every wall, with barometers and tidal clocks and navigation maps crowding for space.

'That's a real captain's armchair,' she said before he was over the threshold. He'd paused to duck under fishing nets, feeling this place was really, really not set up for him.

'Um…great. Which chair?'

'The squishy one between the anchor and the oars. I can take those nautical charts off it if you want to sit down. I'll show you straight to your room for you'll want to wash,' Doris offered, and he suppressed a shudder.

But his room, an attic with a view seemingly all the way to the Antarctic, was blessedly sparse. He had a comfortable iron bed with a ship's wheel etched into the wrought iron, but that was as far as the nautical theme went.

'Susan told me I had to keep the decorations out of this

room,' Doris said disapprovingly as she ushered him in. 'She says men don't like fuss, and I have to say I've had more repeat visitors since I cleared it. I get lots of fisheries people here,' she explained. 'Susan's right. You don't like fuss.'

'Not much,' he admitted. 'So…Susan knows what men like?'

'That sounds nasty,' she said, shooting him a suspicious glance.

'It wasn't meant to be.' Or was it? He hadn't figured Susan out yet.

'She seemed to recognise you.'

'She knew my brother, a long time ago.'

'It must have been,' she said. 'She's been happily settled on the island for years now. Your brother's American?'

'My brother died three months ago. But, yes, he was an American.'

'Oh, my dear,' she said, moving instantly to sympathy. 'And now today. And everything burned. Your car went up with the whole three bridge spans. Burned to a crisp. You'll have had luggage. And a computer, I guess. All you young ones have computers. Susan said I had to get wireless internet if I wanted businessmen here and I have, but if your computer's burned…' She blinked, obviously seeing it as yet another tragedy he had to face.

'And I'll bet you had lovely clothes,' she said. 'Those you're in are ruined. I know, dear,' she said, patting his arm with motherly reassurance. 'You take a nice deep bath. There's a robe in the bathroom for when you finish—I leave one there for my guests because Susan says men like robes. But while you're bathing, I'll do a ring-round and see if we can get you something to wear.' She did a fast visual appraisal. 'Six foot two? Nice and lean, too. One of our fisherman—Nick—he's just your build. Muscular, if you know what I mean. Nick has brown hair, though. Not lovely and black and curly like yours. Ooh, that's lovely hair. It's just like Susan's twins. I tell her they'll grow up to be heartbreakers. Just like you, they'll be, big and tall and dark.

You can see it already. Seven years old, they are, and such a handful. But that colouring…goodness, I'd swear they'll grow up with the same lovely skin and hair that you have.'

He stilled. Everything stilled. Since the moment the boat had crashed into the bridge the day had taken on a surreal air. He felt like the time-line continuum had been smashed at the same time as the bridge, leaving him disoriented and confused.

But he was focused now. Very, very focused.

'Susan has twin boys?'

'Yes,' she said. Doris was fussing with his towels, anxious to extend the conversation. 'Joel and Robbie. They're darlings.'

'I guess they look like their father,' he said, and held his breath.

'Well, we wouldn't know,' Doris said with asperity. 'Off she went, our Susan, just after she'd got the last of her rehabilitation qualifications. Her grandpa lived here, so she spent every holiday with him, but as soon as she finished university she was off to see the world. Mad to go, she was, and who could blame her? There'd never been a penny to bless herself with, ever since that no-good mother of hers dumped her on her grandpa when she was four. Anyway, off she went, and we all thought she was having the holiday of a lifetime. And maybe she did and maybe she didn't, but she came back two years later with two baby boys. She'd done a bit of basic nursing to add to her rehab qualifications, and she said it was because she'd decided to stay here. She's wonderful. We don't know who the twins' father is and we don't care. She's never mentioned him and neither do we.'

'Oh,' said Sam. Faintly.

'You have a nice long bath and get your head together,' Doris said kindly.

'Yes. Yes, thank you. I think I need to.'

CHAPTER THREE

'I'M THINKING I might go away for a few days.'

Susan had arrived at Donna's to pick up the twins. Unfortunately the boys were still swimming with Donna's husband, and Donna knew Susan well enough to realise she was upset. She sat her down, gave her a cup of tea and got straight to the point.

'Why might you be thinking of leaving?'

'We need a break. The twins and I.'

'When did you last have a break?'

'I can't remember.'

'And what happened today…'

'Has nothing to do with it.'

Donna frowned, trying to make sense of it. 'Did you know this guy who crashed the boat?'

'No.'

'And the other one?'

'What other one?'

'The guy who pulled him out,' Donna said patiently. 'The doctor. The one built like a Hollywood movie star.'

'No!'

'Aha,' Donna said, pouncing. 'You do.'

'I've never seen him before in my life.'

'Muriel said you recognised him.'

'I didn't.'

'She said you called him Grant.'

'I just thought he looked a bit like…'

'A bit like someone called Grant?'

'Yes,' she said, and glowered, but once started there was no stopping Donna. Donna and Susan had been at school together, best friends since they'd been four. The friendship had been interrupted while Susie had gone to Sydney to train as an exercise physiologist and Donna had met and married an abalone fisherman from Port Lincoln, but Susie returned to the island at almost at the same time Donna had persuaded her Nick that Ocean Spray would be a wonderful place to base his abalone boat. Two months ago Susie had delivered Donna's latest baby in the back seat of her car, with the car parked halfway across the bridge when said baby had arrived in a desperate hurry three weeks early. Which meant Susie knew almost all there was to know about Donna, but there was a gaping hole in Donna's knowledge of Susie.

A hole which included the twins' conception.

'Is this Grant the twins' father?' she asked now, and Susie shook her head furiously.

'This guy's called Sam.'

'But you thought this guy was Grant.'

'He's not.'

'But you thought he was the twins' father.'

'I think I'd know the twins' father.'

'You're prevaricating.'

'I'm not. I just thought I might take a few days away. Could you run the pilates class, do you think?'

'Are you kidding? I'm still postpartum. Besides if this guy is related—'

'He's not related.'

'To who?'

'I have to go,' Susan said, thumping her mug down with a force that splashed tea onto the tabletop. 'Gladys Holmes needs her leg ulcers dressed. If you give the twins dinner, I'll pick them up later.'

'Sure,' Donna said easily. 'This Sam…'

'Donna.'

'No, really,' Donna said, sounding serious. 'I'm sure he must have swallowed fuel. That was a huge underwater swim.'

'It's nothing to do with me,' Susie said stiffly. 'He refused to go to the mainland…'

'Yes, and he's staying with Doris. You know Doris is a bit deaf. If he wakes up in the night, coughing his lungs out, she won't hear.'

'Serve him right. He should have gone to hospital.'

'Suse,' her friend said. 'I'm shocked. Where's your Hippocratic oath?'

'I'm an exercise physiologist. Not a doctor.'

'He's a doctor, though,' Donna said thoughtfully. 'And a yummy one. Was Grant a doctor?'

'Donna!'

'Just asking,' she said, and grinned. 'OK, sweetheart, off you go and dress ulcers. But don't you dare think of going away. We all might die in your absence. You're the sole medical provider for this island, Susie, and don't you forget it.'

'When do I ever?' Susie said—lightly, she thought—but suddenly Donna looked at her sharply.

'Suse, I was joking.'

'Yes.'

'We can do without you.'

'But not now.'

'Not if you really need to go,' Donna said, and reached out and hugged her friend. 'You know that. But, Suse… Ooh, I wish you'd tell me why.'

* * *

It was her favourite part of the day. Late summer meant it was almost nine when the sun set. The twins, after a long day at school and an after-school swim and dinner with Donna's kids, had collapsed into sleep. Awake they had the combined energy of two small fire crackers, blasting through life, leaving chaos in their wake.

She loved them to bits. From the time she'd first felt them move within her she'd accepted that this was right, that they were meant to be. She adored them. However, that never stopped her breathing a sigh of relief when both of them were asleep.

Grant's children…

How could Grant be dead? And why was his twin here?

She felt limp. Exhausted. Maybe it had something to do with the drama of the day, but she'd responded to crises before without this sweeping sense of exhaustion.

So maybe she had to accept that her fatigue had everything to do with this man. Dr Sam Renaldo, now hopefully safely ensconced at Doris's on the far side of the island.

She'd have to see him tomorrow. Well, that was expected, she thought grimly. She'd always known her past could catch up with her.

Though not in the shape of Grant's twin. She'd expected at some time to face Grant. Indeed, she'd almost hoped for it, for the boys' sake.

But now…It was too sudden, she thought. She needed time to get her head in order.

The swing on the back veranda was gently rocking as she stared out over the moonlit water. This big old house had once been the ferryman's residence. Its rambling garden, full of ancient, weather-gnarled tea-trees, meandered down to the high-tide mark. This had been her grandpa's favorite place in the whole world. 'Where are you when I need you most, Grandpa?' she asked softly, and there was no answer. Of course not.

John Mayne had been ferryman to this small community before the bridge had been built. He'd married young, but his bride had stayed only three months, taking her embryonic child—Susan's mother—with her.

Susan's knowledge was sketchy, but she did know that her grandmother, and her mother after her, had been…erratic? If her grandfather hadn't appeared on the scene when Susan had been four to pick up the pieces, she might well have ended up in an orphanage.

'So I knew from you about disastrous relationships,' she said grimly to the ghost of her grandpa. 'Why I thought Grant was different…'

'Everyone thought Grant was different,' a male voice said, and she jumped about a foot. And then she flinched as Sam Renaldo appeared at the foot of the stairs.

'Hi,' he said, and he smiled exactly as Grant had once smiled. He was mind-blowingly male, as Grant had been mind-blowingly male. Just…gorgeous. But he wasn't Grant. She couldn't make sense of it. Looking at him smiling at her made her feel dizzy.

'Can I come up?' he asked.

'No,' she snapped, panicking. She stood up and crossed to the veranda rail to stare down at him. She felt better standing up. Safer. 'How did you get here?'

'Doris lent me her car.'

'She shouldn't have.'

'Why not?'

'You're recovering.' She sounded grumpy but there wasn't a lot she could do about that. Grumpy was the least of it.

'You got a fright, too,' he told her.

'I didn't have to hold my breath for ten minutes.'

'Neither did I. Two minutes tops,' he said, and smiled again and came up the ten rickety veranda steps two at a time. He was dressed like any islander, in slightly baggy jeans, an ancient windcheater and flip-flops. There was no reason at all for her heart to lurch sideways.

It did. Because of Grant? It had to be.

'Is there any word from Sandridge?' he asked, and that, at least, was easy. This guy was a doctor. She could treat him as a colleague. Maybe.

'They've transferred Pete to Melbourne,' she said. 'He can get specialist attention for the burns there. His wife, Carly, has gone with him. The admitting officer at Sandridge says most of the burns are superficial. He put the flames out himself by jumping in the water, and you did the rest.'

'And you. He'll do much better because we were able to get the wrap on fast.'

She nodded. 'Good for us.'

'And the shoulder?'

'He's going into Theatre tonight to get that sorted.' She glanced at her watch. 'He ought to be in there now. He's in the best hands—the plastics guy who's operating is excellent.'

'So you rang Melbourne to check?'

'Yes,' she said, warily. 'Is there anything wrong with that?'

'No,' he said thoughtfully. 'But it shows you care.'

'Sure,' she said, and he looked at her sideways.

'You're touchy.'

'I'm nervous.'

'Why?'

'Because you're a part of my past I thought was gone for ever.'

'I was never part of your past.'

'No, but you look like—'

'Grant. Yes, we're twins.' He hesitated and then rephrased it. 'We were twins.'

'I am sorry about that,' she whispered, and then couldn't think how to proceed.

This was so disconcerting it felt like a dream—to be talking to Grant and yet not Grant. To be seeing Grant's smile and yet not Grant's smile. This was an older, softer—more world-weary?—version of the man she'd once thought she'd loved with all her heart.

'I guess I'm sorry not just for you,' she whispered at last. 'Grant was an amazing guy. Larger than life, really.'

'He was at that.'

'That sounds…dry,' she said cautiously. 'Almost sarcastic. Didn't the two of you get on?'

'We got on enough.'

'I think I remember Grant talking about you,' she said. 'Are you his only brother?'

'Yes.'

'Then it was you. I asked once. He said, "Yeah, I have an older brother. The conscience of the family." That was all he'd ever say.'

'You were with him how long?'

'Three months.' She bit her lip. It seemed wrong to be talking of Grant. She hadn't talked of him for almost eight years. Grandpa had never asked—he'd tried the relationship stuff himself and had failed dismally so he hadn't been about to chastise her, and it was no one else's business. Was it this man's business?

Maybe it was. If Grant was indeed dead…

'How did he die?' she asked.

'Acute myloid leukaemia.'

Leukaemia. She chewed her lip, feeling a bit sick. 'That seems nuts,' she said at last. 'If you told me he'd been killed paragliding or mountaineering or…'

'Or murdered by a jealous lover,' he said. 'That was always his best-odds option.'

She wasn't going there. 'He got time to think about it?'

'He was diagnosed two years ago.'

'That's dreadful,' she whispered, and turned to look out to

sea. 'Dreadful for you, too. And you're here because... He didn't...he didn't...'

'Want me to contact you?' He joined her at the veranda rail, staring sightlessly out to sea. 'No. To be honest, I needed an excuse to get away from things for a while. Yeah, Grant's death knocked me for six. We fought like hell, but...well, maybe you know enough medical stuff to know how hard the battle against leukaemia is. Anyway, since his death I've had trouble moving on, but I didn't know anything about you until I read his will.'

'His will?'

'He left you—'

'I don't want anything from him,' she said, suddenly furious. 'No way. There's no way he can salvage his conscience by leaving me money. I don't want it and I won't take it. I bet he left money to all his women.'

'You were his only legatee.'

She sucked in an angry breath, not wanting this to be happening. Not wanting this to go one step further. 'I still don't want it. How dare he? Salving his conscience...'

'Did he need to salve his conscience?' he asked mildly, and the anger she felt at that was like releasing a cork from a bottle of shaken fizz.

'You bet he did,' she snapped. 'The bottom-feeding, low-life. I was dumb, dumb, dumb to ever get involved with him. I can't believe he even remembered me after all this time, and if he did I'll bet it was only so he'd get in good with St Peter. I can just see him up there. "It's OK, St P. I paid the girl off. Can I help it if she was a sucker?"'

'Um...' Sam said.

'And you look like him,' she went on. 'You stand there and look like him, and it's a wonder I haven't slapped your face as I've longed to slap his year after year after year. And now he's robbed me even of that.'

She flung herself down from the veranda, brushing through the tea-trees and stalking the small distance down to the beach in front of the house. He followed. For a moment he thought she was going to head straight into the water, clothes and all, but she stopped at the water's edge and contented herself with kicking furiously at the incoming waves, soaking herself in the process.

He stopped at a cautious distance to watch.

'Wimp,' she said, disgusted.

'I know,' he said apologetically. 'But these are the only clothes I've got and Doris will give me a really hard time if I go home wet.'

She'd raised her foot to kick the next wave, but she hesitated a fraction, caught by the pragmatism of what he'd said. 'She will,' she admitted.

Her anger cooled, replaced by…what? She didn't recognise the sensation. She was five yards in front of Sam, staring blindly out at the moonlit sea, and she didn't want to turn back to face him. How could this man look like Grant and not be Grant? She had spent eight years thinking of what to say at this moment and now the moment was changed, made crazy, twisted inside out.

Grant was dead. This was the brother. The responsible one. Sam.

It didn't matter. He looked like Grant and that was enough. She wanted him gone. Or herself gone. She should have fled that afternoon while she'd still had the chance.

'Tell me about the twins,' he said heavily from behind her. 'Your boys. Susan, I need to know. Are they Grant's sons?'

The silence stretched out to eternity. What do you want me to say? Susie thought miserably, and then fear kicked in. After all this time, to have someone suggest there might be a custody claim…

That was dumb. That was pure, illogical terror, for when had there ever been a threat to her boys? There was no power in the world that would allow a claim now. Grant was dead. There was nothing to fear. But she took a long, deep breath, then another, for suddenly it seemed she needed courage to answer openly.

'I have twin boys,' she said. 'Grant is their biological father.'

He said nothing. She turned to face him then but he was looking straight through her, at something she couldn't see.

'Did Grant tell you about them?' she asked, and their gazes met. But now he was looking at her as if she was crazy.

'Did Grant know?' he demanded.

'Know what?'

'That he had children.'

It was her turn to stare blindly at him. Of all the sick jokes…

'Oh, sure,' she said, struggling not to sound bitter. 'I hid it from him so I could keep all the fun to myself.'

'I didn't mean—'

'You don't know what the hell you do mean,' she said, and she walked the few steps through the shallows back up the beach so she could see his face more clearly. 'Sam, why are you here? I'm very sorry that Grant is dead. Believe me, I am. Once I thought I loved him, and I've told the boys he was a fun, loving doctor who went off to save the world instead of being a dad. They'd rather they had a dad but until four months ago they had a wonderful grandpa, and this close island community means they'll never be lost for someone to do the dad bit. Kick a footy. Learn what a razor's for. That sort of stuff. So there's no need for you to feel bad, or feel you need to take a hand. And I don't want money either. I really don't want Grant's money, no matter what he's left me.'

'Why?'

'I told you.'

'That you don't want anything to do with Grant or anything that concerns him. Why?'

'It's none of your business.'

'It is my business,' he said savagely and she took an involuntary step back. Her face gave him pause.

'I'm sorry,' he said, contrite. 'Susan, I'm sorry. I didn't mean to frighten you.'

'Then don't shout. Get in your car and go home.'

'He was my twin,' he said, lowering his voice but not much. 'I can't believe he had children and I didn't know.'

'He barely knew himself.'

'Then you…'

'Not for want of telling,' she whispered, and the anger surged again. 'I left Australia eight years ago and it was supposed to be the trip of a lifetime. I'd just qualified as an exercise physiologist and I got a job in a rehabilitation unit in London. I thought I was, oh, so clever. But I was, oh, so lonely. And then I met Grant. It was Christmas Eve. One of our patients had collapsed and I went up to the ward to see him. Grant kissed me under the mistletoe—how corny's that?—and we were together for three months. Three fabulous months. I couldn't believe we were so happy. Then he asked me to marry him. Oh, we didn't announce it—he was flying back to the States for two weeks and he wanted to break the news to his parents first. That's what he said and I was so dumb that I thought that was fine. I was so in love. So we were getting married and on the nights before he left he asked if we could stop using condoms. Because it didn't matter, he said. And what sort of ring did I want when he came back?'

She choked on the last couple of words, feeling again the anger, the sheer raw emotion of his betrayal.

'But he'd never intended to come back,' she said flatly. 'He just…went and I heard nothing. Three weeks later I rang his parents. Your mother. I knew her number. He hadn't given it to me but…just a crazy whim, I guess, but I'd copied it from his phone. Your mom told me he had a job in New York and he had a darling new girlfriend, and of course she'd give me his work number. If I really wanted it.'

'Oh, Susan,' Sam said, feeling sick. He could hear his mother doing that. She may well have suspected Susan was upset but she'd protect her beloved Grant for all she was worth.

'So I rang him and I told him I was having a baby,' she said. 'He told me to get rid of it and he'd send me a cheque to cover the cost. And you know what? He didn't even do that. Not that I ever would have used it. So I had the twins and I came back here to live with the people I trust. But every birthday and every Christmas I send Grant photographs, hoping, I guess, that as they get older he might crack and let them contact him. But he's never contacted me. He's never said a word. And now...'

'Now he's made you the beneficiary of his life insurance policy,' Sam said, and he named a sum that made her stagger.

CHAPTER FOUR

SHE wouldn't take the conversation further. It was as if the money had formed an impenetrable barrier.

How would she have reacted if Grant himself had come? Sam wondered, watching her face in the moonlight and trying to guess at emotions behind the façade.

Grant had wounded her far more than she'd ever admit. He heard it in her voice, and he saw it on her face.

It fitted with everything he knew of Grant.

Grant had possessed everything—intelligence, looks and charm. His charm had carried him through life with gay abandon. When their parents had split up, their mother's millionaire lover had decreed he could cope with one child, not two. So Grant had been taken, while Sam had stayed behind, caring for their devastated father.

When Grant's results hadn't quite gained him a place in a prestigious medical school, suddenly Grant had become best friends with…well, the right people, and places miraculously opened up.

When their father had lain dying of inoperable cancer, with the hard yards done by Sam and his aunt, suddenly Grant had been there, reaching out to his father, regretting his absence, charming, charming, charming, so the last-minute change in their father's will hadn't been in the least surprising.

That Grant would fill his time in London with a homesick beauty—yes, Sam could see him doing the whole romantic bit. Except a ring, of course, because that would involve monetary sacrifice. And then walking away…Yes, absolutely, that was Grant.

But toward the end of his illness Grant had suddenly thought he mightn't make it. Those last weeks Grant had spent in blind terror. That must have been when he'd made his will. By then he'd gone through all his money, but there had still been an insurance policy paid for by his mother. Maybe he'd left it to Susan only because he'd realised otherwise it would go to Sam. That might be an ignoble thought, but Sam had been sure of it. Now, though…

Now Susie was looking at him with distrust, and he hated it. He hated it that Grant had hurt her. She was so…so….

No. He didn't have a word for it. He'd never met anyone like this woman, and the thought that Grant had hurt her was almost unbearable.

'He really wanted you to have it,' he said solidly, but Susie shook her head.

'He'll have had another agenda. You know I've been broke for years? When I found I was pregnant I knew I had to upgrade my qualifications to basic nursing if I was going to make a living on this island. That meant another twelve months at university before I came home, and it nearly killed me. Grandpa couldn't help. He was on a pension and not well himself. So I worked nights right up till I was eight months pregnant to pay my way. In desperation I wrote and asked Grant to send the cheque he'd originally promised. He didn't bother to reply.'

'I'm so sorry.'

'Don't be,' she said brusquely. 'I have it sorted now. I've managed to scrape together enough to open my little pilates studio, and I have remote nurse status so I can charge for basic medical treatment. There's nothing more I need.'

'And if the boys want to go to university?'

'I'll worry about it when the time comes.'

'You're knocking back security for them.'

'Maybe I am,' she whispered, and she sounded just a little unsure.

'I'm happy to organise the money into a trust fund for the boys,' he said gently. 'If…'

'If what?'

'I have a great-aunt,' he said, thinking it through as he spoke. He'd barely had time to come to terms with the existence of the children himself. The idea that was coming to him now…

'A great-aunt,' she said blankly, and he shook himself, smiling ruefully at her in the moonlight. The whole situation had him off balance, but the way she looked in the moonlight…yeah, off balance was the least of it.

'Sorry. I'm thinking aloud. I'd imagine your brain's spinning as fast as mine. What say we consider our options and meet again in the morning?'

'I'm busy in the morning.'

'Doing?'

'Pilates.'

'I don't understand the pilates.'

'What's there not to understand about pilates?' She sounded almost belligerent and he grinned.

'I'm just an ignorant doctor…'

'Don't patronise me.'

'I'm not,' he said, and swallowed his smile. Which was tricky. She was wearing faded jeans with the knee ripped out of one leg, and a tiny singlet top. She looked like a beautiful, free urchin of the sea.

The sight of her took his breath away. It was doing his head in.

He'd come because of Grant, he told himself harshly. He had no business to be looking at her like he was looking.

'Honest,' he said helplessly, and she glowered.

'Yes, you are,' she snapped. 'You don't know the first thing about pilates but I'll bet you have a whole list of labels in your head in the same category. Yoga. Tai chi. Meditation. Myotherapy. Hypnosis…'

'Hey!'

'Going up the scale till you reach midwifery, physiotherapy, dentistry and ear-candling. All very nice in their way but infinitely inferior to medicine. Your medicine.'

'My Aunt Effie will love you,' he said, and she stopped in mid-tirade and blinked.

'Your Aunt Effie.'

'She's an astrologer.'

'An astrologer.'

'That's someone who—'

'I know what an astrologer is,' she said, putting her hands on her hips and glaring. 'I'm a Virgo.'

'I can see that about you.'

'I bet you don't hold with it.'

'On the contrary, I hold with it absolutely. I had to type up Aunt Effie's astrology charts every month for years while I was a kid. It was the way I got my allowance.'

'But you don't believe it.'

'You see,' he said apologetically. 'Grant and I were the same sign.'

'And you're very different from Grant.'

'I'm the cautious one. Not exciting. Just plain plodding Sam.'

She blinked. 'So diving into pools of burning petrol…'

'It wasn't burning when I dived in, and it was totally out of character,' he said, and suddenly found that he was smiling. Because he wanted to make her smile? Yes, he thought. Damn you, Grant, of all the lousy deceits…

She'd turned and was walking up to the house. He followed,

a yard or so behind, keeping his distance, aware it benefit him to tread warily. Now that he'd thought of Aunt Effie…

'There's no reason for you to stay on the island,' she said, cutting across his thoughts, and he nodded. Reluctantly.

'Maybe not. If we can meet tomorrow.'

'I told you. I have pilates.'

'After pilates.'

'I do house calls after pilates. Come and watch a session.'

'I don't think—'

'Or come and do a session,' she said unexpectedly. 'You have a stiff neck.'

'How do you know I—?'

'I watch how people move. I've watched you. It's not today that's made it stiff, is it?'

'No, but—'

'That's what I thought. Your core stability is all over the place.'

'My core stability is nothing of the sort,' he said, sounding affronted, and she chuckled. It was lovely chuckle, he thought. Nice and rich and throaty. He started to smile back…

The phone rang.

The house was fifty yards from the beach, up a slight incline. By now Sam had figured that the majority of the islanders lived on the far side of the island from the bridge, on Doris's side, on a horseshoe harbour where the fishing fleet was moored. There was a cluster of homes around the harbour, with a few shops, a pub and a small school. The centre of the island was barren, a shearwater colony he'd been told, so the land was a mass of tunnels made by nesting birds, with uncleared bushland in between.

Yet Susie's house was on the side nearer to the mainland, in a spot that seemed almost desolate. Cars going back and forth over the bridge would give some sense of human connection, he thought, but now the bridge was down there was nothing. Away from the lights of the house there was only darkness.

The phone was ringing loudly, an outside peal designed to be heard from much further away than the distance they were from the house. A woman inside the house flung up a window, and peered out.

'Susie?' the woman yelled. 'Are you there?'

'Get it for me, Brenda.'

'It'll be you they want,' Brenda grumbled, but she slammed the window down and the ringing stopped.

'It'll be me they want,' Susie reiterated, trying not to sound relieved. She turned to him and held out her hand, expecting it to be shaken. 'I need to go. Goodnight, Dr Renaldo.'

'I'll see you tomorrow.'

'My pilates class starts at nine.'

'And it finishes?'

'My day finishes about seven. Then I'm committed to the boys.'

'So it's pilates or nothing.'

'It'll do you good.'

'Thank you, but no.'

'Susan?' The window was flung up again.

'Coming, Brenda.'

'Who's with you?'

He watched as Susan hesitated, but she had to answer. 'The doctor who saved the guy this morning.'

'That's really handy.' The woman calling out the window looked extraordinary. She was dressed in a flowery pink house-coat, with a floppy red bow at her neck. Her head was a mass of plastic hair curlers. She was leaning right out of the window, trying to see. 'Can you both go?'

'Go where?' Susie called back in a voice of foreboding.

'There's been an accident on the wharf,' Brenda called. 'Henry's boat's dropped off the crane and Lionel says that Henry's under it.'

'Dear God,' Susan said, and headed up the veranda, three steps at a time.

'It's OK,' Brenda said reprovingly. 'He's not dead or anything. I asked. But Lionel says he thinks he might have broken his arm.' She beamed at Sam, obviously delighted the way this was playing out. 'So if you could take the doctor with you it'd be great.'

'Let me talk to Lionel.'

'He's hung up. He said he had to organise the crane to get the boat off.'

'I'll go,' Susie said, resigned. 'Brenda, can you ring Nick and ask him if he can go down to the harbour as well? I don't want those yahoos playing with cranes.'

'I'll tell them you called them yahoos,' Brenda said.

'You're welcome to,' Susie said shortly. 'Sorry, Sam, but I need to go.'

'Take him with you,' Brenda retorted.

'He may not want to go,' Susie said doubtfully, and Brenda snorted.

'He's here, isn't he? He's got a pulse and he's a doctor. What else do you want? Ooh, Henry will be really pleased if he has a doctor to fix his arm right here.'

Brenda slammed down the window. Susie turned back to Sam. Resigned.

'It's OK,' she said. 'You don't need to come.'

'Why don't I need to come? If this Henry is being squashed by a boat…'

'It doesn't sound like he's all that squashed. And you don't live here. I'm on call.'

'There's no other medical help on the island at all?' he asked, and she shook her head.

'I'm it. But if it was serious, the boys would have told me to hurry. I'm not panicking.'

'Having a boat drop on you sounds serious.'

'Maybe,' she said dubiously. 'But if I gunned the car across the island every time someone said they're dying I'd have hit 'roos and been dead myself these last seven years.'

''Roos?'

'Kangaroos.'

She might not be panicking but she was moving fast, crossing to the garage at the end of the house and hauling the doors wide.

'I'll come,' he said, and she hesitated. Serious or not, being called to a medical emergency when you were on your own would be hard. She was clearly torn.

'I am a doctor,' he said, and she teetered and was lost.

'Thank you. I'd appreciate it.'

Afterwards he thought maybe he should have followed in Doris's car, but his instinct was to join her and she didn't object. Seconds later he was in the passenger seat of the old estate wagon he'd driven that morning. The car rattled ominously as she backed it out of the garage, then backfired as she gunned the motor and headed across the island.

'You like to announce your coming?' he said mildly, and she shrugged. She seemed tense. And why not? he thought. She'd had a rough day. She'd be tired and she didn't know what she was facing. As well as that, having him sitting beside her must feel like she was with a ghost.

'The islanders are taking a collection for a new car for me,' she said briefly, deflecting his thoughts. 'Maybe in a couple of years…'

'So Grant's cheque will come in handy?'

'I won't touch his money.'

'Maybe you need to get your head around it,' he said gently. 'It's not as if Grant's alive to see you throw his money back in his face. Taking a moral stance will only hurt you.'

She bit her lip and retreated into silence. It was a ten-minute drive across the island, and there were indeed kangaroos. He'd seen them as he'd driven this way, grazing calmly on the verge. One had just as calmly leapt in front of his headlights earlier in the evening, so he could appreciate why Susie was driving slowly now.

This set-up was weird.

'If you're the only medic for the entire island, why live on the far side of the island to the rest of the population?' he asked cautiously.

'It's my grandfather's house,' she said. 'He used to be the ferryman before the bridge. I'd like to be in town but I'm hardly in a financial position to swap.'

'I say again—'

'I know what you're saying,' she said icily. 'I need to think about it. Leave it.'

He left it. There was another loaded silence.

'Who's Brenda?' he asked, striving for some neutral topic.

'She's my cousin and my housekeeper. Her housekeeping's pretty erratic—actually, Brenda's pretty erratic—but we love her. And she's great with the boys.' She gave a faint smile, and the atmosphere lightened a little. 'I'd be lost without her.'

'She's colourful,' he ventured, thinking of the bow.

'You'd better believe it. She's the best ballroom dancer on the island.'

'How many ballroom dancers are there on the island?' he demanded, startled.

'Population of five hundred. Maybe three hundred. It's our national sport. Half the reason my pilates is so popular is that my oldies get to dance longer.'

It was so improbable that he grinned. A geriatric fishing community with a penchant for ballroom dancing on the side, propped up by Susan's pilates.

'How many working fishermen are here?'

'Three boats,' she said briefly. 'And only one still working full time. The problem is the bridge. The boys have to land their catch at Sandridge to ensure reliable marketing. Nick's the youngest—he's the guy I asked Brenda to contact. The other two boats are winding down. The whole island's winding down, really. We have a small cheese-making industry. There's a kelp factory. Retirement's big business.'

'Which is where your pilates comes in.'

'That's what I wanted to do full time.'

'Wanted?'

'Before I had the twins.'

'But you can't do that now.'

'The nursing pays the bills.'

'I see.' He didn't, but she wasn't explaining. 'So you live with your boys and with Brenda?'

'If you're asking if there's another man, there isn't,' she said brusquely. 'Not that it's any of your business.'

'I know it's not my business.'

'Good.'

'Tell me what we're likely to be facing,' he said, deciding medicine was a way they could talk without getting too personal too fast.

'I hate to think,' she said, braking as a pair of wallabies decided to cross the road. The wallabies got halfway, paused, stared into the headlights and then loped off leisurely to continue their evening perambulation.

Susie slowed down even further.

'If there's someone seriously ill…' he said tentatively, and she shrugged.

'You think I should be doing lights and sirens? They don't work. If I put a 'roo through the radiator then I walk the rest of the way. The islanders know I do my best. It's the price they pay for living here.'

'Why isn't there a doctor?'

'With a population of five hundred?'

'And now the bridge is down it's worse.'

'We have tourists doing dumb things on the bridge all the time,' she said. 'We're used to being cut off.'

'Why doesn't everyone live on the mainland?'

'Ocean Spray's a great place to live.'

'You're not lonely?'

'There's another of those personal questions. Butt out.'

'Consider me butted.'

She flicked him a glance that might almost have been one of amusement. He wasn't sure. But then he saw her face set again, and a spasm of pain appeared before she had it under control. His appearance was upsetting her, he thought. It was upsetting her a lot.

Suddenly he desperately wished he didn't look like Grant. He wished he'd met this woman for the first time with no strings.

He wished he didn't have Grant's cheque in his pocket.

That was dumb. It meant that he was attracted to her, and that was even more dumb. This sensation of…interest? was only because she'd been Grant's woman, he thought. Grant's death had left an emotional black hole, one he couldn't find the edge of, much less climb out of.

'You and Grant weren't close?' she asked into the silence, and he thought about how he should answer. There was no way but the truth, he decided.

'No,' he said at last. 'Our parents split up. My mother raised Grant, and my father and my aunt raised me. We only got to know each other well…' He hesitated.

'When Grant became ill?'

'Yes.'

'That's none of my business either,' she acknowledged. 'But he only ever talked of you as…'

'Someone he didn't like much?'

'I never knew he had a twin. I imagined you older.'

'Three minutes older.'

'Hardly enough to turn you into the domineering presence he inferred.'

'We had an issue with my father's estate,' he said bluntly.

'You mean he didn't get it all?' she asked, and he blinked at that. He'd been so accustomed to being cast as the villain of the piece that her calm assumption of Grant's likely greed left him speechless.

'He wasn't all bad,' he said at last, and she gave a hollow laugh.

'Hey, you're talking to the woman he proposed to just so he could make love to me without precautions. Don't defend the indefensible.'

'OK,' he muttered, and that felt bad, too.

'It's damned if you do and damned if you don't,' she said with sudden sympathy. 'Half of you wants to hate him because he was a cheating, lying low-life, and the other half still thinks of him as he could be, charming and fun and…alive.'

'Yeah,' he said morosely, and they both stared straight ahead.

'You're on leave?' she said suddenly.

'I… Yes.'

'Since Grant died?'

'Maybe.'

'Because it hurt so much?'

He hesitated. It was hard to explain, his reasons for taking extended leave. But there was something about Susan's quiet enquiry that made him try.

'I just couldn't do it,' he said after a while, wondering what it was about this woman that made him need to talk. 'We fought so hard for his survival. I donated bone marrow. We fought with everything we had, yet still we lost. And now…I'm an ortha-paedic surgeon, but every patient I see…seventy-year-olds with advanced rheumatoid disease, joints diseased with age…it's doing my head in.'

'You're angry at his death?'

'It just seems such a damned waste,' he said savagely. 'And Marilyn…'

'Marilyn?'

'My ex-fiancée.' He gave a rueful smile. 'Don't look like that. Marilyn and I were colleagues first, lovers second. She's been supportive but by a month after Grant's death, when I hadn't moved on, she was increasingly resentful. There was a Chair in the Orthopaedics department I was aiming for, and when I lost interest Marilyn lost interest. So here I am. I guess I'm depressed and I'm self-treating by travelling. But as far as loving Grant…'

'Maybe we should start a club,' she said softly. 'The Grant Renaldo Love to Hate Club. I wonder how many members we'd pull in.'

'Lots,' he said flatly.

'So I wasn't the only sucker?'

'Maybe you're the only one that ended up with children. But, yes, he hurt a lot of people.'

'Including you,' she said sympathetically. 'I'm sorry.'

'How can you be sympathetic after what he did to you?'

'I can't hate him completely. He gave me the twins.'

'He messed up your life.'

'Maybe. But who's to say I would have been happier if I hadn't met him? Maybe I'd have met someone else, maybe in London.'

Then she shook her head. 'No. I guess I would have had to come home anyway. At least this way I had the chance to get the additional nursing training.'

'That's something else I don't understand.'

'You see, I knew the island,' she told him, speaking softly, and he knew she'd made a conscious and a difficult decision to talk. 'My initial plan was to base myself in Sandridge but to come back here part time and do exercise rehabilitation—there's such a need among the elderly here. Then when I found I was pregnant I panicked. I knew I'd be here full time and there was no medical service. Once I had twins I wouldn't be able to go back and forth to Sandridge as I'd planned, so I decided to provide as full a service as I could. So I did another year of training to get basic first aid under my belt. It nearly killed me to do it, having the twins in the middle of it, but I was determined. I came back here when the twins were twelve months old and now I'm set for life.'

'So the pilates is going well?' he said cautiously, and she smiled and relaxed a little.

'It is. A huge percentage of the population are over sixty, and on the use-it-or-lose-it principle I've talked them into pilates. We're doing fine. Doris is a case in point. When I came here she was struggling to use a walking frame. Now she's running her own bed and breakfast and bossing every tourist she comes into contact with. She's not quite ballroom dancing again but we're working on it.'

They'd reached the little township now. They passed Doris's place on the headland and Sam thought again he should have followed in his own car. But Susie hadn't suggested it. Maybe subconsciously she did want to talk to him, he thought, and then he thought that maybe that was wishful thinking.

Wishful thinking? Did he want her to relax and talk to him?

She'd been his brother's girlfriend. She was the mother of his nephews.

There was a thought from left field. Nephews.

He needed to phone his great aunt, he decided. Aunt Effie would be…flabbergasted?

'I'm sorry to ask this of you,' Susie said, and he hauled himself back to the here and now.

'You're sorry?'

'Brenda suggested that you come. I had no right to expect you to. But…'

'It's a huge responsibility to be sole medic for the whole island,' he ventured, and she grimaced.

'I didn't think it through properly before I came,' she admitted. 'When the bridge is out, when something happens and immediate help's needed, then I'm it. Brenda's right. Having a doctor, even if it's just for tonight, is a blessing. So I'm saying thank you very much in anticipation for what you're called on to do tonight. I know you've been trapped into doing it, but it helps.'

CHAPTER FIVE

THE harbour front looked dark and deserted. This was a working harbour, Sam saw, taking in the situation as Susie parked the car, but there wasn't much working going on tonight. There was a small cluster of pleasure boats—small cabin cruisers and yachts—tied at the wharf but the big pens were empty.

'The fleet went out tonight,' Susie said briefly as she manoeuvred the car as close as she could to the dock. 'Prawning's started.'

'So who's Henry?'

'An ex-bank manager with the seamanship of a newt. One of a trio of ex-financiers who think they know everything. I've lost count of the number of times Nick's been called on to get them out of trouble. What the hell's he done now?'

And then she saw. They both saw.

A crane was at the far end of the wharf, where a single overhead lamp cast an eerie glow through the sea mist. The crane was linked to a boat, a sleek, fibreglass cruiser a little smaller than the one that had nearly killed Sam that morning. It looked like the crane had been used to haul the boat out of the water and swing it around over the jetty so the hull was accessible to work on. But things hadn't gone according to plan. The boat's stern was still dangling from the crane's cable, but there was a chain dangling free. Snapped. The bow was almost on the ground.

There were two elderly men standing back, their faces showing collective relief at Susie's arrival.

'That's Ted,' Susie said briefly as she climbed from the car. 'Retired accountant. And Lionel. Retired financial advisor. Morons both. I bet they've left him stuck under there.'

They had. As they approached they could see a man pinned by a shoulder underneath the hull, gazing out at his mates with despair. But he didn't look in agony and he didn't look like the whole weight of the boat was on top of him.

It looked as if he'd been scrubbing the hull when the chain had snapped. There'd been a pile of tools in a crate close by. The crate was now partly crushed, but it formed a wedge of smashed wood, taking the brunt of the boat's weight.

But the guy was still obviously trapped, and obviously in pain.

'Suse,' he gasped as he saw her. 'I thought you'd never get here.'

'You didn't think,' Susie said carefully to the two onlookers in general, 'to get the damned thing off him.'

'We were worried it'd slip more,' one of the men said.

'Did you call Nick?' she demanded.

'Donna said he's out,' Lionel told her.

'If Nick's the fisherman, then prawning's started,' Sam said mildly. 'I guess that means we're on our own.'

She bit her lip. 'You distracted me,' she muttered. 'I should have thought…' For a fleeting second she closed her eyes but when she opened them she was in control again. Ready to do what she had to do. She moved forward with purpose but Sam gripped her shoulder, tugging her back.

'No.'

'What do you mean, no?'

'Wait. You know the drill, Susie. First rule of a medical crisis—check that there's no external danger. There is here. Wait.'

'I can't—'

'Wait! Is there anyone else you can ring to help with the crane?'

'Yes, but—'

'Then do it.'

He made sure she had the message—that she wasn't about to defy him—then moved to the end of the boat, carefully assessing the whole situation. He hauled a crate forward, climbed up and tugged the chain holding the stern of the boat up. It seemed solid.

But one chain had snapped. This one would have almost double the load. If one could snap, so could the other.

'He's hurt,' Susie said. She'd made a fast phone call and he knew she was finding it almost impossible to stay back. The guy trapped under the boat looked pale and ill, but he was still talking. A trapped arm didn't make it a life-or-death situation where risks were reasonable.

'We'll get this thing propped up first,' he growled.

'Henry's in pain.'

'And we're no good to him squashed. What did you say about not rushing across the island in case we hit a 'roo? You had it right then. Henry, we'll get you out as fast as we can but we're getting decent props under the boat first. You want to tell us what happened while we work?'

'I can tell you what happened,' Susie muttered.

'Help me with this first,' Sam said. He strode toward the far end of the jetty, where a group of large oildrums stood in a row. He spun one round, dropped it and rolled it toward the boat. 'Help me,' he ordered. 'Get these drums under the boat. Now.'

They worked fast. Lionel and Ted weren't completely useless—once they were given a job to do they joined in with gratitude. Sam had them rolling every drum there was over to the boat. There he set them up lengthways on their sides, facing the boat, wedging eight drums along the width of the jetty. There was a six-inch wooden ledge at either side of the jetty, so once in line the drums couldn't move.

Once he had them more or less in line he shoved them forward, inching them tighter, using all his strength to push them hard in against the sloping hull, so hard that the tension eased from the remaining chain. Once there they forming a solid wedge that meant if the chain snapped, the boat couldn't fall further onto Henry.

Then he ran another line of drums behind to back up the first row. If the boat dropped now it might even take the weight off Henry—it certainly would no longer crush him.

Only when he was sure the thing was done would he approach Henry, and he didn't let Susie near even then.

Henry had lain and watched in silence, helpless but seemingly reassured by Sam's decision. When Sam finally dropped to his knees and came in beside him he groaned in relief.

'So let's see the damage,' he said. 'Susie, what about formal introductions?'

'Henry, this is Dr Renaldo,' Susie told him, thinking she ought to be under there and not Sam. To be extraneous in this sort of crisis felt wrong. 'Sam, this is Henry Martin. Henry's obviously been lying under his boat to clean it rather than put it into dry dock. Which is dumb, not to mention illegal. It costs five bucks a day to use the dry dock, so he'll have waited until the fleet's out to use the crane while no one's watching. Henry, are you out of your mind?'

'Five buck is five bucks,' Henry said defensively. 'Glad to meet you, Doc.'

'You would have let Susie come under here without props if I hadn't come?' Sam asked mildly, and there was an awkward hush. Of course they would have, he thought grimly. Susie was the reliable one.

Like he was. The recognition was suddenly piercing. Good old Susie, here to pick up the pieces. Like good old Sam, picking up Grant's pieces.

Only in Susie's case it was for a whole island.

He had to move on. 'Level of pain, Henry?' he said. 'On a scale of one to ten.'

'Seven?' Henry said cautiously, and Sam nodded.

'Let's get that right first. Susie, do you have any opiates in that wonder bag of yours?'

'You should be used to the contents of my bag by now,' she said, and he heard her smile. She fetched it and would have brought it to him but he stopped her with a curt order.

'No. Push it over to me.'

'It's safe now.'

'It won't be safe until we have him out of here.' And they needed to do that fast, he thought, noting the sheen of sweat around Henry's eyes, feeling his pulse, worrying.

Henry must be well over seventy. They needed to get things settled before his heart reacted to the strain.

There was a good pulse in the wrist of his trapped shoulder. The blood circulation wasn't compromised, but there was still a fair weight on his shoulder.

'Is there someone coming to help with the crane?' he asked.

'Yes,' Susie said. 'The cavalry. A couple of retired fishermen. Oldies but goodies, unlike some here I could mention. Five more minutes tops.'

'I'll give you morphine while we wait,' Sam told Henry, and Henry's eyes widened.

'Can you do that?'

'If Susie says I can.'

'Help yourself,' Susie said. 'You're the doctor.' She let out her breath in a sigh of relief. 'And you have no idea how good it feels to say that.'

And then the cavalry arrived. Two men who were as old as Henry and Ted and Lionel, but who carried the scars of a lifetime of being out in all weathers.

These guys were good. They summed up the situation in seconds, hauled chains from the back of the truck they'd arrived in, one of them climbed up the crane and attached the new chain, they hooked it to the collapsed end of the boat and two minutes later the whole load was raised.

The moment the boat was high enough Sam and Susie hauled Henry clear. By now the morphine was kicking in, enough for Henry to raise a small 'Hooray' as he emerged.

He could well say hooray. He'd been incredibly lucky.

Once clear of the boat they were free to examine him properly. As Sam ran his hands over Henry he thought it had been little short of a miracle that the guy hadn't been killed.

'I'm thinking that shoulder's just dislocated,' Sam said, feeling it with care.

'Will I still have to go to hospital?' Henry quavered.

'I'll ring the coastguard,' Susie snapped, relieved that the drama was over but still terse.

'I could possibly put it back in here,' Sam said and she frowned.

'Without X-rays?'

'It seems a simple dislocation.' He met Henry's anxious stare. 'I'm an orthopaedic surgeon,' he told him. 'I do know what I'm doing. Susie, do you have any muscle relaxants in that magic medical kit of yours?'

'What sort of relaxants?'

He named a couple of drugs and she nodded. 'It's set up as a dispensary so I can give stuff on doctor's phone orders.'

'Well, then,' he said. 'I've treated hundreds of dislocated shoulders in my time. What are we waiting for?'

And ten minutes later it was done. He pulled down and forward, the bones slid smoothly back into place and the white-faced Henry was almost back to normal.

'Thanks, Doc,' he whispered as the onlookers raised a small cheer.

'Think nothing of it.'

'Lionel will drive you home,' Susie said.

'I'll drive myself home,' Henry said, sounding offended.

'You try and your car keys are going to the bottom of the harbour,' Susie snapped. 'You have more than enough drugs on board to put you straight to sleep. Show some sense for once in your life. Oh, and expect a bill from me, from Dr Renaldo and from the guys I've had to call out. Next time you want to save yourself five dollars, Henry Martin, you do it on someone else's patch.'

And that was that. They drove back to the other side of the island in silence. Susan was so tired she was ready to drop. It was close to midnight. It was dumb that she'd let Sam ride in her car—if he'd followed he could be at Doris's right now and she'd be driving home and things would almost be back to normal.

Except how could things be back to normal now Sam had arrived?

If only he didn't look like Grant.

Was that the only problem?

There was also the issue of having thought she'd left the past behind her. Although she'd sent photographs of the boys to Grant, she'd long since accepted he wanted nothing to do with them. Their upbringing was her responsibility. Well it still was, but this man's presence unnerved her.

He was silent now. He'd be tired, too, she thought. This morning's drama would still be taking its toll. He'd risked his life today. A man didn't do that without questioning something deeply fundamental within himself.

Or did he? What would she know about men? She was working on the example of her grandpa. Maybe Grandpa alone wasn't representative but then enquiring further had landed her with Grant, and she wasn't going there again.

But she shouldn't categorise this man according to Grant. It wasn't fair, even if they did look so alike it made her edgy. He wasn't like Grant. He'd taken over tonight, taking the responsibility from her shoulders, making her feel almost light-headed with relief.

He wasn't like Grant. He was responsible. He was practical. He was seriously skilled.

He was…gorgeous.

'Are you OK?' she asked cautiously into the stillness, and he glanced across at her as if her question had surprised him.

'I'm fine.'

'When did you land in Australia?'

'Five o'clock this morning.'

'You're kidding.'

'No.'

'You got straight in a car and came here?'

'It's only five hours.'

'You're nuts.'

'I wanted to get it over with.'

There was another silence at that. Lots of unanswered questions.

'You wanted to hand over the cheque and run,' she said at last.

'There didn't seem much point in hanging around.'

'There doesn't,' she said, carefully extending his meaning. 'So you'll be leaving tomorrow?'

'I'd imagine it might be difficult to replace my hire car and get off the island.'

'Anyone with a boat will take you.'

'You mean Henry.'

'I think our Henry might be feeling a bit sorry for himself for a day or two. But there's always someone ready to row for cash.'

'I thought you said we were headed for bad weather.'

'Motor for cash, then.'

'I get seasick,' he said. And then he hesitated. 'No. Susan, I want to meet the twins.'

Here it was, then. That which she'd most feared.

'They're nothing to do with you,' she managed.

'I still want to meet them. I believe it's my—'

'Right?' she finished for him, her fears growing. 'What right would that be?'

'They're my nephews.'

'Grant's never acknowledged them.'

'He has. By sending you this cheque.'

'Then you can rip it up now,' she snapped.

'No.'

'It's not buying you rights.'

There was a pause. A regrouping while they both figured out where they stood.

'I'm sorry,' he said at last. 'That was clumsy.'

'You have no rights.'

'No,' he said, sounding humble.

'And if I don't want you to meet them, that's my right.'

'Yes,' he said.

She cast him a suspicious look.

'I mean it,' he emphasised. 'But I would very much like to meet them.'

'Not tonight.'

'I'd imagine they'll be asleep. Possibly in the morning?'

'They'll be at school.'

'Do you have school on Saturdays here?'

'Oh.'

'I just want to meet them, Susan,' he said gently. 'It's not the end of the world.'

'No,' she whispered. They were pulling into her yard now, beside the big dilapidated house with the verandas all round. There was a single light above the back door but the rest of the house was in darkness. It was a solitary life, he thought. Stuck here...

'I love it,' she said and he blinked.

'I didn't mean...'

'No,' she said. She pulled to a halt and climbed out before him, then stood and watched as he climbed out. The car was between them. She backed. No closer.

Maybe it was just as well. For she made him feel...

She made him feel...

'Thank you for helping tonight,' she said, taking another step back toward the veranda, her body language a clear 'now-go-home' message.

'I'll see you tomorrow.'

'If you want,' she said. 'You're welcome at pilates class.'

'You don't seriously expect me to do pilates.'

'You don't seriously expect to stay hurting from that stiff neck?'

'No, but—'

'There you go, then,' she said, and she walked up the veranda steps and opened the back door. 'Nine tomorrow. Wear something comfortable.'

'There'll be a local shop that sells gym gear, then?' he asked dryly.

'Whoops,' she said, and then her face brightened. 'Nick, a fisherman here, plays football. I know his wife. Nick'll lend us some shorts.'

'Nick's already lent me clothes. And...us?'

'Nick and Donna will lend me the shorts because they're my friends. You can wear them,' she said graciously. 'I expect he lent you the first lot out of charity.'

'Thanks very much.'

'Think nothing of it,' she said chirpily. 'Nine o'clock it is.' She turned and walked into the house and closed the door behind her.

Leaving him outside.

He had Doris's car. It was right beside him. He had the keys. He should go.

Instead, for a moment he just stood there. He saw the lights go on inside. Susie appeared at her bedroom window briefly before her blinds were snapped down.

If he didn't move soon he'd be arrested for stalking.

He went. But very slowly. Wary of 'roos. Wary of potholes. Wary of exhaustion taking its toll.

Or just plain wary. Because what he was feeling was very strange indeed. He was in uncharted territory.

Susan had been his brother's lover. It should make her out of bounds.

No. She'd had a brief affair with his brother eight years ago. That should make no difference.

So what he was feeling was OK?

He didn't know what he was feeling. That was the whole trouble. It was like he'd looked at her and his world had tilted sideways so he wasn't sure what was up any more.

It was jet-lag, he told himself. Exhaustion. Shock.

It was none of those things.

It was Susan.

He'd gone.

That he'd hesitated had made her very nervous indeed. That he hadn't driven straight away; that he'd watched her walk inside; that he'd seen her light flick on...

It was too personal and she didn't intend getting personal with Sam Renaldo. With any Renaldo for that matter.

She was comparing him to Grant, she thought bleakly. She shouldn't. Sam was different.

Which was exactly what she didn't need to think, she told herself, suddenly breathless. She'd been down that track a long time ago and she had no intention of setting her feet in that direction again.

Sam was in his car now. She listened as he backed out the drive and disappeared across the island. Silence settled over the old house like a thick grey blanket.

That was another thing she wasn't allowed to think. That this place was too quiet and too tied up with the past and too…dull?

'I've had my excitement,' she told herself, and went into the twins' room, just to check.

They were, as they always were at this time of night, curled up in sleep, her lovely, freckled, brown-eyed cherubs who'd taken over her life eight years ago and had ruled it ever since.

'I don't regret a minute,' she whispered, but she knew it wasn't quite true. One short love affair and wham, she'd become a single mother with twins. And somehow, wham, she'd also become sole medic for this island. Eight years ago she'd gone to London to see life. Well, life had kicked her straight back here.

She was content. She usually was content, she corrected herself. It was just tonight…

Having Sam sit beside her…Having Sam's help with the medicine…Having Sam smile…

It was a different smile from Grant's. Grant had referred to Sam as his older brother and he did seem older.

Well, that was a no-brainer, she told herself, trying to keep some sense. It'd been eight years…

But it wasn't the years. It was the way he smiled. Grant had been out for whatever life had thrown at him. He was larger than life, a party animal, someone who could pull you in and make you party whether you wanted to or not.

Sam seemed gentler. Sadder?

Duh, he'd just lost his twin.

No. Just different.

She was getting mawkish. She was smiling to herself in the dark, thinking about Sam's smile—and that he was Grant's twin and had she lost her mind completely? Let's just put the hormones in the cellar and lock the door for the duration, she told herself harshly, and she walked forward and tucked the bedclothes more firmly round her little boys.

'You're a mother and you're medic to this island,' she said firmly, out loud. 'You have no space for hormones in your life, so get over it.'

But she stood still. She was no longer gazing at her twins.

She was seeing Sam's face. Grant's face?

Who would know? Get over it.

She was gorgeous. Mind-blowingly, earth-shatteringly gorgeous.

Sam lay in Doris's little attic room and stared at the ceiling and all he saw was Susan.

Susan's face surfacing inches from his in the water, her glorious hair splayed around her.

Susan tonight, kicking at the waves in the shallows, telling her story.

Susan scolding the men, rolling the oildrums with ferocity and determination, Susan furious yet deeply concerned.

No wonder Grant had fallen for her.

Yet…had Grant fallen for her?

No, for how could he have ever done what he'd done? The thought of his twin's actions made him feel ill. To deliberately risk pregnancy, to prey on a girl alone and vulnerable, to promise marriage with no intention of ever committing…

That had been Grant all over. He hadn't deserved to be loved by her. He'd surely never loved anyone.

As Marilyn had said, it was dumb to feel Grant's death as deeply as he did.

Yet he and Grant had been twins. They'd been together

every moment until they'd been five years old and when they'd been split up, the five-year-old Sam had grieved so much he'd made himself ill.

Had Grant?

He didn't think so. Realistically? No, it had all been about Grant.

He'd hurt Susan so much.

Well, reparation, at least in part, was possible. Grant's life insurance money was the one asset Grant hadn't been able to touch, and because he hadn't wanted Sam to have it he'd bequeathed it to Susan. It had been the right gesture for the wrong reason. But it would at least atone…

Nothing would atone for what Grant had done.

What was it the shrink had said? 'Your mother and Grant hurt your father so much that you've spent your life atoning for them. You need to figure out that your life is yours, Sam. Yours.'

Yeah, that was deep. It was also true. So he had to move on, head for that holiday he'd planned, traveling round the world until he had his head in order.

He needed to get to know Susan.

No, he told himself harshly. Susan was a part of Grant's past and nothing to do with him. He had to give her the cheque and move on.

But he needed to meet Susan's twins.

Yeah, he conceded. He did. And then he had to get the hell out of here.

Right. Tomorrow.

CHAPTER SIX

'GET those hips up, Lionel.'

He wasn't coming. Hooray he wasn't coming.

'I thought the doc was supposed to be coming this morning.' Ted, the ex-accountant, was looking particularly un-accountant-like. Tight bike shorts, a chest-hugging singlet and a sweatband were designed to make him look manly. He was little, skinny and a lifetime of sitting behind a desk had left him almost without a muscle to call his own. But he was doing his best. He was concentrating really hard on his upright rows, wobbling as the weights of the pulleys proved too much for his aged arms.

'Well done, Ted, you can go a bit lighter now.' Susan grinned to herself as she took the weights down. From one kilogram to five hundred grams. Any lighter and she'd be pushing the weights herself.

Ted took another pull. He wobbled dangerously to the side and she righted him.

'Concentrate,' she growled.

'We can't concentrate after last night,' Ted complained. 'I'm still feeling shaky.'

'I should be shaking the lot of you,' Susan said, glowering. 'Were you out of your collective minds?'

'It's only a small boat,' Lionel said placatingly. 'And you know we have to watch every cent.'

'Like you're not all rolling in money,' she said. 'You spend your time in here discussing the best way to organise your investments, so don't give me that rubbish. Henry has more money than he knows what to do with—you all do—and you begrudge five bucks. I should get Dr Renaldo to charge Henry specialist rates. Callout rates for a US specialist. I bet that'd be more than five dollars.'

'You know, it'd be good to have a doctor like him here permanently,' Lionel said sagely, judging, rightly, that it was safer to move on from last night's fiasco. 'Do you reckon we should ask him to stay?'

'He's an American. He's here to visit.'

'He's here to visit you, Susan,' Lionel said thoughtfully, with a sideways wink at Eric.

'How do you guys get your information?' Susan demanded. 'Right, Lionel, your weights are going up.'

'It'll be bad for my heart if my weights go up.'

'Have half a kilo less butter on your toast every week,' she said. 'Don't be a wimp.'

'You're a hard woman,' Lionel said. 'But I was sure Doris was saying he'd be here today.'

'When were you talking to Doris?' She shouldn't ask, she thought. It was wrong to encourage island gossip. But…

'Donna took Nick's footy gear round to Doris,' Lionel said. 'You know Doris is Donna's aunt? And Donna wanted to know what was happening. So Doris told her and Bert just happened to be round at Donna's, chopping wood, which he does every morning when Nick's at sea..'

'All right,' Susan said, seeing their sideways glances at each other and thinking, Uh-oh, she'd opened Pandora's box. 'It doesn't matter.'

'No, but you're interested,' Ted said. 'She is interested, Lionel. Donna said she'd be interested.'

'Ted…'

'It's about time you had an interesting male round here,' Ted said. 'A hot-blooded young woman like you.'

'I'm not in the least hot-blooded,' she snapped.

'Aren't you?' a voice asked, and she whirled to the door.

He was there. Sam.

He was a different Sam again. A Sam dressed in football shorts and a jersey with the sleeves slashed out. Nick's football gear. Of course. Part of the island network. Susan wouldn't have been surprised if Donna had been right behind Sam, pushing him into the room.

It was just as well she wasn't. Her friend knew her well, and what she'd make of Susan's mounting colour…She could feel her cheeks burning. She put her hands up to hide it, trying desperately to sound—to feel—normal.

'Do you have to sneak up on me?'

'I thought I was booked in,' he said, casting her an amused look. 'Nine-thirty?'

'Nine-fifteen,' she snapped.

'You ought to sound encouraging,' Ted said sagely from behind his weights. 'Otherwise he'll get the wrong impression.'

'I'm sure I don't mind what impression Dr Renaldo gets.'

'But you want him to do exercise,' Lionel said, shocked. 'You want us all to do exercise. Start him off gentle, like. Five minutes on the exercise bike.'

'Fine,' Susie managed, and motioned to the treadmill. 'Five minutes it is. Resistance high. Uphill.'

'You want to kill him?' Ted demanded, astounded, and Sam grinned.

'I concur. Do you want to kill me?'

'It'd take more than an exercise bike to kill a Renaldo,' she snapped—and then she heard what she'd said. The colour drained from her face. 'I…Sam, no. I'm so sorry.'

'Don't be,' he said gently, and then he took pity on her. He crossed to the bike. It was set up so the user was looking out the window, down to the bay. He set the controls—obviously he'd used one of these before—and started pedalling.

Susie was left to get her breath back.

Why had she said that?

He wasn't Grant. The more she knew him the more she instinctively knew that he was as different as it was possible to be. But he looked like Grant. He had the same smile—the smile that had done her head in. Or her heart in. She was darned if she was going to let her heart be swayed by that killer smile.

So use your head. He was here professionally. So act professionally.

'Um…I need you to fill in a medical form,' she said, sounding awkward.

He pedalled on.

'You can stop for a bit,' she told him.

'I haven't done my five minutes.'

'No, but if you drop down dead and I haven't asked for your medical history, you can sue me.'

'I promise I won't sue.' He kept on pedalling. 'If I'm dead.'

'Your relations could. Your wife?' Oh, help. Where had that come from? She just knew her old men were chuckling.

'No wife,' he said, pedalling on. 'Just one aunt. Aunt Effie. She won't sue either.'

'Get off the bike,' she told him.

'But—'

She put her hands on his handlebars and met his gaze full on.

'Stop,' she said.

He stopped. They were left staring at each other like…like…

'Across a crowded room,' Lionel said in satisfaction from behind them, and she blinked and made a recovery. Sort of.

She grabbed her clipboard from the desk and handed it over. With a pen.

'Fill it in,' she said.

'Yes, ma'am,' he said, and sat back on the bike, pedalling easily and writing while he pedalled.

'Get on with it, you lot,' she told the rest of her clients, and they all grinned and got on with it.

He was enjoying himself.

Once the dreaded medical form had been completed Susie set him on a course of exercises designed to stretch, extend, loosen. He hadn't tried pilates before—when had he ever had time? But now…He was pushing himself, he realised. There was no impact, no breathtaking exertion, just ongoing stretch, extend, stretch, extend, centralise…

He was aware that every one of his three fellow exercisers—and Susan—were watching him, but there was enough in the programme for him to lose himself.

'My shoulders were stuffed until I started doing this,' Lionel told him.

And Sam thought, Yeah, he could feel it doing him good.

Marilyn had bullied him into getting a massage while he'd been on holiday but he hadn't been able to relax. Here, though…This was stretching his taut muscles in a way a massage couldn't, and he found that the intense concentration required for Susan's imperative—core stability—took him out of his head. The stresses of the last few days—hell, the last few years—faded a little.

Faded a lot.

He worked steadily through the list Susan had prepared for him. As each exercise finished she demonstrated the next. She was lithe and free and seriously skilled, fluid in her movements, swinging up and down from the benches, hauling the pulleys with ease, rolling her body, showing him what she wanted him to do.

She was beautiful.

She was also seriously professional. She watched him every step of the way as he started a new exercise. She watched them all. There were only four in the room but that was all she'd be able to manage for she never took her eyes off them.

'I think you can push that trapeze higher,' she told Lionel, and Lionel groaned but then smiled, almost shy, as Susan put her hands under the small of his back and supported him until he had the height she wanted.

Then she did the same to Sam and he smiled, too. She wasn't a big woman. She was as thin as a whippet, with a lean, lithe strength about her. She was wearing crimson leggings and a bright yellow crop top. Her flaming hair was braided. She looked…she looked…

'Don't push it so hard,' she said softly to him. 'This isn't a contest. I want you to think about where your spine is. I'll take the weights down until you get it right.'

He blinked. *This isn't a contest?*

It was a pretty amazing statement. A class where there was no compulsion to get better…

No. There was a compulsion here to get better, but it was to get better on his own terms. He was no different from Lionel, or Ted, or Eric. They were senior citizens and he was still in his thirties but they were concentrating exactly as he was concentrating.

They were doing extraordinary things with their bodies, he thought. Use it or lose it…These men would still be agile when they were a hundred if Susan had anything to do with it.

She had music on the sound system. Some 1970s classics. It wasn't something he'd ever thought he enjoyed but he was enjoying it now. Susan was toe-tapping as she moved between them. She'd put aside her embarrassment at his presence, he thought. She'd forgotten…

'Breathe,' she ordered, and he blinked. OK, he'd forgotten. All this and breathing, too.

'It takes a bit of concentration but you'll get there in the end,' Lionel said kindly. 'It just takes time.'

Yes, he thought. Time.

Did he have…time?

And then it was over. The men were finishing up, doing something they called walking—extending their calves as they lay and pushed against weights—then tugging on shoes, bidding Susan goodbye, joshing each other about how much they'd done.

He'd get to talk to her now, he thought, but he hadn't finished the list of exercises she'd given him.

He didn't need to finish. He swung himself upright and she looked disapproving.

'You're not done.'

'I don't need to—'

'I'm charging you,' she told him. 'You may as well get your money's worth.'

'How much are you charging?'

She told him and he almost laughed. 'That's crazy.'

'I'm worth it.'

'You're worth much, much more.'

He'd taken the wind right out of her sails. She stood there, glaring, but suddenly she was uncertain.

She wasn't very old, he thought suddenly. Five minutes ago she'd been a self-assured, health professional doing a damned good job, knowing what she was doing was good.

Now she looked suddenly lost.

'Don't,' she whispered.

'Don't what?'

'Be nice to me.'

'Why—?' But his words were cut off by a series of insistent raps on the door.

'Mum. Mummy, Mummy, Mummy. We counted and they've all gone now. Can we come in now?'

She cast him an uncertain glance—and then shrugged and opened the door.

What could a man say when his world stopped?

His did. Right there. Right then.

The two little boys had been leaning on the door, pushing, and as Susan opened the door they fell. They hit the floor like a pair of over-excited puppies, rolling, giggling, pushing each other, then tugging each other upright while exchanging insults.

'I told you what'd happen if you pushed.'

'I didn't push.'

'You did. And you've messed my neckcloth.'

They were dressed in what looked like Scout uniforms— khaki shorts, short-sleeved shirts and wide, carefully tied neck-cloths. A baseball-style cap sat off-centre on one head. Another cap lay on the floor.

They looked so like Grant that they took his breath away.

They looked so like himself.

Sam had photographs of himself and Grant when they had been five years old. That was the last photo he had of the pair of them. He'd kept that photograph close for years as he'd grown up. These two boys were two years older, but that was the only difference. The similarities were…terrifying?

'Maybe you'd better sit down,' Susan said.

He thought, Yeah right. He must have lost colour. It was like he was seeing ghosts.

Real ghosts.

The boys had seen him now. Or one had seen him, then punched the other to bring his presence to his twin's attention.

It was so much the action he and Grant had used to each other, over and over, that it made him feel even more weird.

'Boys, this is Dr Renaldo,' Susan said.

'We thought you were finished,' one of the boys said.

'This is Joel and Robbie,' Susan said, and then she took pity on him a little and added, 'Joel has more freckles on his nose than Robbie.'

'I'm pleased to meet you, Joel. Robbie.' He put a hand out and received two solemn handshakes in turn.

'You're an American,' Joel said, with interest.

'Yes,' he said.

'Our dad's an American,' Joel told him.

'We've never seen him,' Robbie added.

'Do you know our dad?' Joel asked.

'I guess that's why I'm here,' Sam said uncertainly. He hesitated. But then he thought, Hell, there was no way around this but through it. Susan would have to tell them at some point. Why not him?

But it was her call. He cast an uncertain look at her and got a sharp little nod of assent for his pains. Go ahead, the look said, but I don't have to like it.

'I did know your father,' he said softly. 'And that's why I'm here. Your father's just died.'

There was a stunned silence. The boys stared up at him, open-mouthed. And he thought…maybe he'd just made a really big mistake.

He should have talked this through with Susan. To just come straight out and say it…Of all the insensitive…

He glanced at Susan, appalled. But she was made of sterner stuff than he was. She assimilated the situation in an instant and decided to make the most of it. She gave him an almost imperceptible nod. Keep going, her nod said. This is your call.

His call. They were looking up at him, waiting for more information, slightly shocked but not so much that they looked distressed. The notion of a father must have been a distant, un-attached concept.

'When did he die?' Robbie asked.

He could do this, Sam decided. When all else failed, fall back on the truth.

'Three months ago. But he was ill for a lot longer before that. He had a disease called leukaemia.'

'Is that why he didn't come and see us?' Joel asked.

'Maybe it was,' Sam said. And then added, more honestly, 'I don't know.'

But it seemed that his answer had been deemed suitable. The boys looked at it from all angles, before coming up with more questions.

'Did you come to tell us he was dead?'

'Yes. I thought your mother should know.'

'Does that make you sad?' Joel asked, looking at his mother in childish concern. 'Are you sad he's dead?'

'I am sad,' she said gravely.

'Did you cry when you found out?'

'I cried a lot a long time ago. I guess I'm all cried out.'

'Sometimes you cry when you think we're not watching,' Robbie said with the perspicacity of the very young. 'Is that because our daddy was sick?'

'I guess…it must have been,' she said.

'You're the doctor that pulled the man out of the burning boat,' Joel said, obviously deciding that his father's death had had all the attention it deserved and now it was time to move on.

'Yes,' Sam said. 'But your mother helped. She's a brave lady, your mother.'

'Mum helps everyone,' Joel said dismissively. 'All the time.'

'You're lucky to have her as a mother.'

'Yeah, but it'd be better if she had more time,' Joel said.

'Mum, Sea Scouts is off 'cos it's too rough on the east side of the island and Mr Fraser says there's an oil slick on this side from yesterday's crash and there's stuff in the water. And none of the kids from the mainland can get here. Mr Fraser sent us home but Brenda's gone over to Mrs Ludeman's for a gossip.'

'I'll ring her and ask her to come home,' Susie said. 'I have two house calls to do before lunch.'

'Pete's dad was going to take us to the beach after Sea Scouts,' Joel said, sounding mournful. 'To practise soccer. But they're stuck on the mainland, too.'

'Go and kick the soccer ball round in the backyard until Brenda comes,' Susan told them.

'We did that,' Joel said, exasperated by the stupidity of adults. 'We kicked it until we saw your clients leave. But we're bored of kicking by ourselves.' He turned his attention to Sam. 'Can you play soccer?'

'Yes,' Sam said before he knew he was going to say it.

'Really?' He suddenly had their absolute, undivided attention. Followed by suspicion.

'Like Mum says she can play? She can kick pretty good but that's all. Even we can tackle better than she can.'

'Americans don't play soccer,' Susie said, sounding stunned.

'There's a generalisation,' he said. 'Like all Australians play the didgeridoo. I had a couple of close Italian friends at university. They let me practise with their team. Sometimes I even got to play in their matches.'

'Wow,' Robbie said. Suspicious, but tinged with real hope.

'Can you come and show us?' Joel asked.

It was the natural sequel. Tell the kids you can play soccer and they'll want you to show them. But...

They were Grant's kids. They were twins. They were so closely aligned to him...

He didn't know them. And Susan didn't know him.

He glanced at her, uncertain, and the doubts in his own mind were mirrored a thousandfold on her face.

'Dr Renaldo's busy,' she said.

'He doesn't look busy,' Joel said. 'Or do you have to do house calls with Mum?'

'Do you need me to come on house calls?' he asked, and Susie's eyes widened.

'No! I mean… No. I have a couple of elderly people I help with showering.'

'You're the only nurse on the island?'

'Yes.'

He frowned. 'So how do you get a day off?'

'Mum doesn't have days off,' Joel said. 'But she says it keeps the wolf from the door. The wolf keeps coming and coming, every time one of those red letters comes in the mail.'

'Dr Renaldo doesn't want to hear about our wolves,' Susie said, sounding desperate. 'And he doesn't want to play soccer either. You'll have to come with me while I work.'

'No,' the boys groaned in unison, and Sam had to grin. He could remember making just such theatrical groans.

Such a long time ago. When he and Grant had still been friends.

'I'm happy to play a bit of soccer with the boys,' he said diffidently and Susan flinched. The look saw on her face was one of pure pain.

'I'm sorry,' he said. This was like stepping on eggshells. He had no idea where to go. 'I didn't mean…'

'No, it's all right,' she said. 'I'm sorry. It's just…well, it's fine for you to get to know the boys. You should. You are their uncle.'

If he was saying things without thinking, he wasn't the only one. He watched panic wash over her face as she realised what she'd said, and the two little boys gazed up at him in astonishment.

'Are you our uncle?' Joel breathed.

'I guess… Yes, I am.'

'That means you're our dad's brother,' Robbie said, squinting as he tried to work it out.

'Yes,' he said gently, flicking a concerned glance at Susie. This was happening too fast. Maybe they should have seen a counsellor or something. This was huge stuff to lay on these kids. To do it without thinking…

But it was done and it couldn't be undone.

'Do you look like our dad?' Joel asked, entranced.

'Um…yes.'

'Are you his big brother or his little brother?' Robbie asked. Robbie was obviously the quieter twin. While Joel pelted Sam with questions, Robbie was edging sideways to stand beside his mother. His attitude was just slightly defensive. Or protective?

Grant and Sam. Grant, noisy, extrovert, demanding. Sam coming behind, picking up the pieces.

'We were twins,' Sam said softly. 'Just like you.'

There was a moment's silence. More than a moment. It stretched on and on. Susie was looking bewildered, lost. Her hand went down to Robbie's shoulder and held.

'Did your twin die?' Robbie asked at last.

'Yes,' Sam said, for there was no other answer.

The boys looked at each other, appalled. And then Joel moved, darting across the room to stand by his brother. He grabbed Robbie's hand and held it fast.

'They're old,' he said, his voice wobbling a little. 'We won't die.' And then he looked at Robbie, his eyes suddenly brimming with tears. 'You're not allowed to die.'

Yep, he should have consulted a child psychologist. Susie was kneeling, hugging the boys to her, and he watched her reassuring them and things twisted inside him. He'd hurt them. He'd hurt her.

Damn Grant, he thought savagely. How could he just have left them? How could he have loved this woman and deserted her? How could he have known that somewhere in this world were twins in his image, and this woman caring for them on her own, and done nothing?

He watched them, an outsider, and he thought, no, Joel wasn't like Grant. Joel was hugging his twin and his mother fiercely. Grant would never have done that. He'd been born without the loving gene.

It was a dreadful thought. Maybe it was a consolation of thoughts, he decided. It was something he'd learned over the long years of being Grant's twin but had never faced properly until now.

Grant had done such damage, to this little family most of all. And now…To hand over Grant's cheque and walk away…

He couldn't, and neither did he want to. To be able to help was a privilege, he thought. To hand over the cheque and know it would help with Susie's metaphorical wolf… To help a little…

If Susie allowed him to, it would be a privilege.

And the thought was like sunlight coming through fog. For months now life had been grey. Maybe for longer. Maybe for years. He'd been fighting for Grant's life as they'd faced leukaemia, but maybe it had been longer than that. For Grant had never been able to figure it out. That love…helped.

'The disease that your dad got was really, really rare,' he found himself saying. He was still standing awkwardly above them. Susie was crouched, holding her boys close. 'It's called leukaemia. Sometimes when adults get leukaemia they die. But when kids get it…you know what? Kids nearly always get better. So I think we can guarantee that you won't die of leukaemia.'

It wasn't quite true, he thought. There was a chance in a million that he'd be called a liar, but that chance was so small that for now the important thing was that they accept it as the truth and move on.

'You're a doctor,' Joel said, sniffing and turning from the safe circle of Susie's arms. 'You make people better.'

'Just like your mother,' Sam said, and smiled.

'But you couldn't make my dad better.'

'We've talked about that,' Susie said gently. 'Sometimes it's just people's time to die. Mostly it's when they're really old. But sometimes it's because they have dreadful accidents like Mr Coutts when his house caught on fire. Or when they get a really bad disease like your Dad had. But mostly it's 'cos they're old and they've finished living their lives. That's why we should have lots and lots of fun when we're young. So, yes, you and your Uncle Sam can go play soccer.'

Uncle Sam. The name hung over all of them. It was a brilliant ploy, thought Sam, and he smiled at Susan.

And then she smiled back.

Wham.

How the hell had that happened? One minute he was concentrating on life-and-death matters and traumatised children and then…She only had to smile.

Her eyes were still moist. Her smile was a bit tremulous, a bit wary, but still…He'd never seen such a smile. It knocked him sideways.

'You're our Uncle Sam?' Joel asked, and he had to haul himself out of Susie's smile and think of an answer.

'Um…yes. I guess I am.'

'Cool,' Joel breathed.

'Uncle Sam's American,' Robbie said.

'That's right. I'm American.'

'There's a picture of an Uncle Sam in Tom Adams's poster book,' Robbie said, eying him doubtfully as if he suspected he was being duded with an imposter. 'He has a big hat on with red, white and blue stripes and he's saying, "Your Country Needs You."'

'I guess there's probably more than one Uncle Sam in the world,' Sam said weakly.

'And you really can play soccer?' Joel said, getting back to the important issues.

'Yes.'

'Can you take us to Whale Cove? That's the best soccer-playing sand. The rest is too small when it's high tide.'

'He can play with you here,' Susie said.

'It's too small here,' Joel objected.

'Can I take them to Whale Cove?' Sam asked. Then as he watched her face, seeing myriad conflicting emotions, he said, 'OK, maybe it'd be better to stay here and play.'

But then Susie almost visibly came to some inner conclusion, some really difficult decision.

'No. It's OK. You can all go to Whale Beach.'

'Will you bring lunch over?' Joel said.

'And our togs?' Robbie added.

'I don't have time.'

'You promised you'd take us swimming at lunchtime,' Joel said, wounded.

'I'll bring you back,' Sam said gently, seeing Susie close to panic.

'No,' she said, and she rose and squared her shoulders. 'I can do this. I'll bring lunch across.'

'It shouldn't be an ordeal,' Sam said, and he had to force himself not to reach out, not to touch her, not to somehow make contact. For that was what he wanted.

Not…Not for him, he thought, startled at the direction his thoughts were heading. But for her. He wanted to reassure her. He wanted to comfort her.

Yeah, and the rest, he thought, stunned. And that was dumb. She was terrified now. How to make it worse? Try and get physical.

One step at a time.

And there was another dumb thought. Where did he want this to go?

He simply wanted to get to know his brother's kids, he told himself. That was all.

'Do the boys know the way?' he asked.

'We do, we do,' the boys yelled in unison.

'Then let's go,' he said, and smiled at Susie. 'Is there anything we need to do before we go? Do you want us to stop at the store and buy something for lunch?'

'I don't need anything,' she said, sounding breathless. 'Except…'

'Except?'

'Except for you to stop smiling,' she snapped. 'It's driving me crazy.'

CHAPTER SEVEN

THEY were still playing soccer when she arrived.

Whale Cove was a tiny secluded inlet on the north of the island. The cove was only a couple of hundred yards wide, but the incline to the sea was slight, meaning there was a vast sandy swathe before the water—an ideal soccer field—and the water was shallow until far out. The beach closest to the tiny island town was good too, so most of the locals didn't bother to get into the car and come here, but this had been a favorite fishing spot for Susie's Grandpa. She'd spent half her childhood here.

It was home.

Once, when she'd been young and had fancied herself in love, she'd thought of bringing Grant here. Now there was the echo of Grant here, playing soccer with her sons.

Except...this wasn't Grant. An echo? A pale replica of Grant? No way.

They hadn't seen her arrive. The road rose to a steep bank before the cove, so she was looking down at the game being played out on the beach below.

Sam was good.

Soccer was an island passion, more important even than ballroom dancing. The few children on the island lived and breathed soccer, and the adults watched it on television with the almost religious fervour of the truly committed. Once the island had fielded a team in the mainland competition, and it was a source of immense sadness that there were no longer sufficient young men to carry on the team's proud history.

All of which meant that Susie knew her soccer. So she knew now that the ball skills Sam was showing were seriously good. She watched him kicking the ball back and forth to each of the twins in turn, adjusting the ball between each pass with deft foot juggling. She was very, very impressed.

And now she had a giant case of hero worship on her hands, she thought as she watched her boys struggle to perform to Sam's standard, trying out his moves, giggling with pleasure as he progressed around the sand with the ball bouncing up and down on his head between passes.

A comic.

She'd never have thought it of him. Yes, she'd only known him since yesterday but he'd seemed…sad? Well, he would be, she thought. He'd just lost his twin.

But…How close had they been that Grant could bequeath his money to her and never tell Sam of his sons' existence?

For Grant must have known about the boys. She'd checked over the years, not wanting to send information to old addresses. Grant's mother had told her the hospital where he'd been working. She'd checked every year before sending updated photographs. Often Grant had moved on but there'd always been a forwarding address they were willing to give her.

So Grant had seen his sons, yet he'd shown no interest. Now here was Sam, making her boys fall in love with him.

In love…

The thought came from nowhere. Goodness, she was overreacting, she told herself. One morning's soccer. But she looked down at them, three crazy kids together.

Sam…

Oh, for heaven's sake. Here she was, reacting like a moon-struck teenager. 'That's the sort of behaviour that got you into trouble in the first place,' she muttered fiercely to herself, and collected the picnic basket from the back seat of the car, collected her common sense from down around her ankles, and headed down to the beach to join them.

They saw her coming when she was halfway down the track. They were still her kids, she thought as they abandoned Sam and the soccer ball and whooped up the track to meet her.

And that was a dumb thought, too. How could she imagine that her kids were any less hers because this stranger had appeared? He had no claim on them, neither would he want any. He'd be nice to them for a little, give them a helpful vision of who their father was and then disappear.

Leaving her financially secure.

That was something she hadn't got her head around yet. The cheque that Sam had presented her with would make all the difference.

They were tearing up the path now, her two rascal kids she loved with all her heart. She set down the picnic basket and braced herself, but still staggered as they hit her full on.

'He's the best…He can really play…Did you see him pass? Did you see me kick? I nearly got it past him. Mum, you should see him pass!'

They were delirious with happiness and she found herself grinning with them as Sam followed them more sedately up the track.

He stood looking down at the boys, his smile slightly crooked as if he wasn't quite sure what had caused the mass hysteria. 'You'll strangle your mother if you hug her so hard,' he said mildly, and the little boys whooped as if he'd said something really funny.

'Get the picnic rug from the car,' Susie told them, disengaging herself, dusting herself off and straightening. Then as the boys tore away she smiled up at Sam.

'Thank you,' she said simply. 'That's wonderful.'

'What?'

'They love soccer. I'd like to take them for decent coaching but there's never time.'

'They're pretty good for seven.'

'Yeah, well, we practise a lot.'

'We?'

'I can kick a mean soccer ball.'

'You're kidding.'

She grabbed the soccer ball, wheeled and kicked it down toward the beach. There were two straggly trees right at the end of the track, at most a couple of yards apart.

She kicked it neatly between them.

'Someone wiser than me said women need to do everything twice as well in half the time to be considered the equal of their male counterparts,' she murmured, dusting sand off her hands in a brisk, businesslike manner. 'Luckily, that's not so difficult. Right. Lunch.'

'You and Robbie against me and Joel first,' Sam said, challenging her.

She looked up into his laughing eyes and thought, no, this is really dangerous, don't do this. But she already knew it was too late.

It was a wonderful hour and a half. To Sam's astonishment Susie's boast had not been an idle one. He'd played at a high level—there was no threat to him if he put his mind to it—but Susie's skills meant that their beach challenge was incredibly satisfactory. She obviously practised with the boys for hours. How many mothers did that for their kids? he wondered. And then thought, How many single mothers did he know? Not many. Those he knew were harried and hard-working. So must Susie be, yet as soon as she'd set the picnic basket down and lifted the ball her cares had been thrust aside.

She whooped with the boys, giggling, shouting, exhorting, yelling and high-fiving with Robbie when they scored against Joel and Sam, and groaning in mock hair-pulling frustration when there was a goal scored against them.

Then hunger called and the soccer ball was put aside and lunch was attacked with the same enthusiasm. She'd made it herself, he thought, and this was no gourmet's delight. She'd sliced a loaf of bread thickly, then made chunky sandwiches with beef and salad three inches thick. They ate them lying full length on the rug, while gazing up at the few white clouds scudding over the sun-drenched sky. The kids and Susie did this often, he thought as he watched them. She had a twin on each side of her. They were content just to concentrate on the serious business of eating. Conversation wasn't necessary.

He was jealous.

It took a few minutes before it kicked in but when it did it almost took his breath away. He'd never had this. His parents' marriage had been dysfunctional. He'd never been sure how they'd managed to conceive at all, and they sure as hell hadn't wanted to raise them. Grant had been raised by a succession of au pairs, usually girls with very little English, out to have a good time rather than care for their charge. Sam had mostly been raised by Aunt Effie.

It didn't matter now. Hell, he was thirty-six. What was the use of aching for a childhood he'd never had?

It wasn't that. He was aching for Grant.

He'd taken his sandwiches a little apart, so he could sit on a rock and survey Susie and the boys from a distance. The little boys were lying dreamily on either side of their mother. While he watched, Susie finished her sandwich, then sat up to fetch herself another. Before she lay down again she kissed each freckled nose in turn.

The boys giggled. Grant would never have giggled, he thought. Grant would have been tugging Susie, saying, 'Look at me, look at me,' unable to bear that attention be paid to anyone but himself.

He felt sorry for Grant.

That was such a blasting thought, coming from nowhere, that he stood up and walked, unable to stand still, thinking it through.

Sure, Grant had been sick. Sure he'd felt sorry for Grant when Grant had been so ill. But before…

He'd always assumed Grant had felt right with his world. Grant had been in control. Yes, his twin had been selfish, but he'd got what he'd wanted.

But now…He turned and looked at the little group on the sand and thought, Grant, you missed this. You could have had it. You stupid, messed-up piece of grief.

'There's room on the rug if you want.' Joel had obviously been watching and was keen to make sure all was right with everyone. 'It's cool to lie on your back and watch the clouds. Mine's a crocodile.'

'A crocodile?' Sam said cautiously.

'Mine's a bunch of balloons,' Susie said. 'That's all I can manage today.'

'Mine's a bulldozer,' Robbie said in satisfaction. 'I reckon I win.'

'We see things in clouds,' Susie said, taking pity on his confusion. 'You look up and see what you can see in the clouds, then if you can make everyone else see it then you win. But bunches of balloons don't really cut it.'

'Lie down and see,' Joel said, obligingly. 'Mum, move over.' Then, as she didn't move, he sighed over the obstinate ways of grown-ups and rolled his little body over his mother and his twin so he was on the outside edge against Robbie and there was a gap right beside Susie. 'Lie down and look,' Joel commanded. 'But can you pass the sandwiches first, please?'

So Sam passed the sandwiches and lay right beside Susie and looked at clouds. The rug was a wee bit too small for the four of them and Susie's body was touching his, just lightly, but touching for all that. Susie's body tensed as he sank down beside her. So did his. But it couldn't last. No one could stay tense for long here. The food was great. The sun was warm on their faces, and the conversation was fun.

They discussed Joel's crocodile and decided they were impressed. They discussed Susie's balloons and Sam was polite but the twins were scornful. They discussed Robbie's bulldozer and judged him the winner.

'Unless you can find something else,' Robbie said, but he sounded anxious.

Sam looked skyward while he munched another sandwich—when had he last eaten this much lunch?—and decided that all he could see were bulldozers, crocodiles and clouds. Nothing else.

'Then Robbie's today's champion,' Susie decreed, and rolled over, kissed her son on the tip of his nose and then peeled off her T-shirt. Then her jeans. Underneath she was wearing a faded red bikini. A seriously gorgeous faded red bikini. Maybe it was only seriously gorgeous because Susie was in it, Sam thought. 'Who's for a swim?' she demanded, and Sam had to blink and haul his attention away from one very small bathing costume.

'Don't you drown if you go swimming on top of a big meal?' Sam asked cautiously as the twins leapt to their feet and headed for the water, but Susie grinned and shook her head.

'There speaks a truly well-trained physician, I don't think. Cramps after lunch went out with whalebone corsets. Coming?'

'I don't have trunks.'

She wrinkled her nose. 'That's right, all your luggage went the way of the car. Will insurance pay for new ones?'

'I suspect burned swimming shorts are the least of the expenses my insurance company is facing,' he said morosely.

'You've lost your computer, too?'

'Doris has already sympathised about my computer.' Gee, her bikini was…was…

'Hey, I'm not sympathising,' she retorted. 'I think anyone going on holiday with a computer needs their head read.'

'I wasn't coming on a holiday.'

'Why were you coming?'

'To see you.'

She considered that. Her lovely body was blocking his sunlight. Her shadow was falling over him and the sensation was somehow intimate. He shaded his eyes to look up at her and felt even more deeply the sensation that his world was being twisted.

He was being stupid. He'd met this woman only twenty-four hours ago. She was the mother of his nephews. To feel…as he was feeling was stupid, stupid, stupid.

'You didn't come to see me,' she said, reasonably, seemingly unaware of the sensations chasing themselves round his head space. 'You only needed to put the cheque in the post. Or were you wanting to see what sort of a mercenary wench your brother had been involved with in his shady past?'

It was so much what he had been thinking that he found it hard to answer. What had he expected? He'd seen some of the women Grant had been involved with over the years and they had always been…well, not like this. Not like Susie.

It was the most beautiful bikini…

'You could have posted the cheque,' she said again, softly. Insistently. She needed an answer.

'I wanted to meet you.'

'Why?'

'I've lost all of Grant,' he said, forcing himself to think as logically as he possibly could. 'I wanted…'

'To see if there was any connection left?' Her face softened in sympathy. 'I can understand that. And it must have been quite a shock to find the twins. Twin echoes of Grant.'

'They're so much not like Grant,' he said slowly, thinking it through.

'Why not?'

'They care,' he said softly. 'Already I can see that. They love you. They love each other.'

'They surely do that,' she agreed, and turned to watch them. They'd surged into the water and were now splashing in a furious display of who could get the most water in the air.

'You've done a great job,' he said, and she smiled.

'I have.'

'You should be proud.'

'I am.'

'And you will take the cheque?'

'Yes,' she said, turning back to look down at him. 'I will. I thought about it all morning and decided that as long as there's no strings attached…'

'There can't be any strings attached. It's straightforward. But…'

'There has to be a but,' she said, and sighed.

'It's just…I would like to be able to see them.'

'You have no—'

'No right. I know that. I'd never ask that they leave the country or anything. But…' He hesitated. 'I rang my great-aunt this morning. My great aunt Effie practically brought me up and she's devastated at Grant's death.' He hesitated, but then he shrugged. This woman was practically family. Why not let it all out?

'She blames herself for the way Grant…for some of the things Grant did,' he said. 'It's dumb but there it is. She's saying she should have been more forceful—she should have stood up to my father and made him intervene and stop the way my mother indulged Grant. It's dumb but it plays with her. I'd love her to meet the twins, and see that Grant's left a legacy of more than distrust and dislike. Seeing Joel and Robbie…I suspect it'd be better than a truckload of antidepressants.'

'You're using my sons as a prescription?'

'Maybe,' he said, and he smiled. 'Better than a bottle of pills any day.'

'But a few more unpredictable side-effects,' she said absently. 'Um…when?'

'As soon as she can organise flights. Susie, I'm holding no gun to your head,' he said gently. 'But I'd love Effie to meet them.'

There was a moment's silence while she thought about it. He half expected her to shake her head, to back away. There was a large part of her that wanted to do just that, he thought. But she didn't. Instead, she became thoughtful.

'So you'd stay here until Effie arrives?'

'If I can. It'll take her a while to organise time off…'

'From being an astrologer?'

'She's a busy lady,' he said, and he smiled. 'But she'll want to come. If it's OK with you.'

'Maybe it is. If you'll agree to a swap.'

'Pardon?'

'I have four elderly islander people who are bedbound,' she said. 'Once a week the mainland doctor comes across and does house calls, but he hates it. Last week he said he was having trouble with his car and didn't come. Now the bridge is down there's no way he'll come, even if I beg. But these people all need comprehensive assessment. I can't change drug regimes myself.' She eyed him assessingly. 'Maybe you can.'

'I can't treat patients here.'

'You're a doctor.'

'Yes, but I'm not registered to practise in Australia.'

'I can get you registered in two minutes,' she told him. 'We've always been classified as remote. Now the bridge is down we're classified as really remote. Really remote means if we can verify your training then the government will let you practise yesterday. I have Dan Mullins with cancer of the oesophagus and suffering pain I can't control. I have Claudia Miller with advanced Parkinson's and I need to adjust her medication but I don't know how. I have Ray Fifer whose leg ulcers are beyond me and Roger Carmichael who's miserable and I'm sure has just got piles, but there's no way he'll let me look.'

'You want me to treat them all?' he demanded, astounded.

'I'll do the hands-on treating,' she said. 'I always have and there's no need for me to stop now. What I want is for you to stand back and give me directions. Oh, and as you and Effie will be seeing my twins for free, you won't be charging Ray and Roger and Dan and Claudia. Right?'

It seemed he had no choice. She stood, smiling pertly down at him in her little red bikini. He would have agreed to anything. 'Right,' he said, dazed.

'Great,' she said briskly, smiling. 'That's sorted. Do you want a swim before we start?'

'When do we start?'

'After the swim.'

'I'm not—' he started, seriously startled.

'If you're going to quibble,' she said, sounding exasperated, 'then I can quibble, too. I know you're not registered but I can take each of your suggestions—you are going to give me suggestions—and then I can run them past Doc Blaxson on the mainland, who has to be the laziest doctor in the known universe. He can OK them. Which he will because Doc Blaxson will do anything for a quiet life.'

'You interfere with his quiet life?' he queried, stunned.

'Too right I do. All the time. But even I can't force him to take a boat over here to where I need him. But now that's sorted. I've solved my medical dilemma and we only have another forty minutes before we need to take the boys back to Brenda. OK?'

There didn't seem to be a lot of choice. 'OK.'

'There you go, then,' she said, beaming. 'So, swim?'

'I only have this pair of pants.'

'Nonsense,' she said bracingly. 'Our first call can be to Ray and he's just your size. A house call in return for dry pants is a good deal, don't you think?'

'Um…'

'There you go, then,' she said again, and she reached a hand down to tug him to his feet. He was so surprised that he let her pull him up. And then…

She'd been laughing. The tone had been brisk and business-like, but she tugged and he rose too easily, guided by her hand, letting her take part of his weight, surprised into letting her do the tugging. He rose and his feet braced unwittingly against her feet.

He ended up right before her. Really close.

Really, really close.

She staggered back and he caught her. His hands gripped her waist and held. Momentarily her breasts pressed against his chest. She fitted against him as if she belonged there. The sensation was indescribable.

She felt…she felt…

Her skin was warm and soft and supple. Her hair had blown free; it was wafting around her shoulders in a flame-coloured cloud. She was wearing her lovely crimson bikini and nothing else, and he held her and the sensation hit him that he'd never held, he'd never seen, he'd never experienced anything, anyone, quite as lovely.

Susie.

'No,' she said, and stepped back, and he made no move to stop her. Even though he wanted to. Things were happening here that he had no control over—that he had no idea what to do with. He could only look down into her lovely brown eyes and know that her own confusion was mirroring his.

'I'm sorry,' he managed, and she took another step back.

'I…It's OK. I pulled you. Are…are you coming in for a swim?'

'I think I will,' he said. The water would be cold, he thought, and that was reassuring. When all else failed, take a cold shower.

'I don't want…' she said, faltering, and he knew what she was saying.

'Neither do I.'

'That's good,' she said, and gave a decisive little nod. 'Because there's no way…no way…'

And then she shrugged. 'I'm sorry,' she whispered. 'I'm not talking sense. As if you'd want…' Her colour mounted and she backed up a couple more steps and wheeled away.

'I'm going swimming,' she called over her shoulder, and she ran down the sand toward the twins as if she was being chased by demons.

He hesitated. Susie raced down the beach and dived into the first wave, swimming strongly out to a buoy a hundred yards from shore. The boys whooped and gave chase—they swam like little seals—but halfway to the buoy they stopped as if simultaneously struck by the same thought, then turned and trod water while waiting for him to follow.

He was wearing borrowed clothes. But the sun was too warm to be comfortable, the translucent shallows beckoned and the boys were waiting.

Susie had reached the buoy. She held onto it lightly while she watched, waiting to see what he would do.

He shouldn't. It was asking for trouble.

He shrugged and abandoned his doubts. He hauled off his shirt and hit the waves with the same sureness as Susie.

The twins headed straight back to him, and when he surfaced there they were, two beaming faces, bobbing in the waves, welcoming him into their world.

'Race to Mum,' they said and off they went, and again he was left to follow if he wanted to.

Susie was waiting.

He did want to. He put his head down and swam with confident strokes. The twins had a ten-yard lead by the time he started. He expected to reel them in but they reached Susie well before him. The boys beamed their pleasure as he finally joined them. Susie was smiling, too, but she looked a little unsure. Maybe very unsure. This was uncharted territory for both of them.

'Race to the rocks at the other end of the cove,' Joel pleaded.

Sam looked where he was pointing and thought, How well could these boys swim?

'Maybe we'd better give Sam a head start,' Susie said.

'You're kidding me.'

'We're seriously fast,' she warned.

'I can swim—'

'I never said you couldn't.'

'I can swim fast,' he said, and tried to glower, which was a bit hard with water dripping into his eyes and Joel and Robbie splashing each other from either side of him.

'Right,' Susie said. 'Let's see you strut your tail feathers. Are we ready, everyone? One, two, three…go!'

She beat him.

He beat the twins but only just.

He surfaced, gasping, and Susie was laughing at him and he nearly choked.

She looked…she looked…

'The honours are mine,' she said smugly. 'You did manage to beat the seven-year-olds.'

'You guys live on the beach.'

'Yes,' she said kindly. 'And we're younger and fitter.'

'Hey!'

'You want a rerun?'

'When I get my breath back,' he gasped and she grinned some more.

'OK, boys, let's leave Dr Renaldo here like a beached whale, recovering his breath, while we go swim a few more miles.'

'I think we should go start work,' he gasped. 'Medicine's easier.'

'It is,' she agreed, teasing. 'And I'm sure a bit of medicine could help you. Come back to my pilates class and we'll get a bit of core strength going.'

'There's nothing wrong with my core strength.'

'No, Doctor. Whatever you say, Doctor,' she said meekly. 'Let's go, boys, and see if the good doctor can keep up.'

CHAPTER EIGHT

SO SAM settled in and immediately found himself busy. Which he didn't mind. It'd take Effie a few days to get here and he may as well do something useful. The alternative was to take a boat to the mainland, find himself another hire car and come back when Effie arrived.

But he didn't want to leave. The rays of light filtering through the fog of his depression were getting longer.

He'd been severely depressed. Sam had accepted that, even if he hadn't been able to fight it. The shrink had suggested medication but Sam knew that there were things going on his head that somehow he had to come to terms with in his own way, and medication wasn't going to help.

But this helped. Being on the island helped. Spending time with the twins helped.

Spending time with Susie helped most of all. The dreary lethargy he'd been functioning in for the last few months somehow lifted when he saw her, when he heard her chuckle, as he watched her move patiently, with skill and with care, among the islanders she obviously loved.

He'd agreed to work in exchange for Effie's visiting rights. It had started as something of a joke but he soon discovered that Susie was absolutely serious. With the bridge down there was no access to a doctor without taking a boat to the mainland and then a taxi to the clinic a few miles south. For ill patients that was a big ask, and Susie had no intention of putting her friends through it while she could make use of him.

On Saturday afternoon he saw four bedbound patients. On Sunday he saw six more. By midday Monday Susie had his temporary registration through and he could prescribe medications without the OK from another doctor. Therefore Susie deemed a clinic would be in order. She did a fast phone-around, and suddenly he had a list of eight patients waiting to see him.

'How many access visits to the twins am I paying for?' he demanded, startled, and she grinned.

'I bet Effie will want to see the boys often. I reckon you should get as far into credit as you can.'

Why not? he thought, bemused, and picked up his patient list and studied it. Haemorrhoids. Shingles. Leg ulcers. Indigestion. Constipation.

'I'm an orthopaedic surgeon, you know,' he said mildly.

'I know.'

'I suspect you know more about how to treat these patients than I do.'

'Maybe I do,' she agreed. 'But I'm not a doctor.'

'Would you have liked to be a doctor?' he asked, and was surprised by a flash of longing in her eyes that she fought fast to disguise.

'There's lots of stuff I wouldn't mind being.'

'Did you get the marks to get into med school?'

'I… Yes, but there was no money. It's no use wishing for what you can never have.'

He thought of Grant. He thought of the unprincipled means Grant had used to get his medical degree.

And this girl…

Hell.

'Do you know how to treat haemorrhoids?' she was asking, moving on, and he was forced to move with her.

'I believe I might. If I can check the pharmaceutical lists before I see the patients—and if I have the internet to hand.'

'Well, what more could we ask of our island doctor,' she said admiringly. 'OK, Dr Renaldo, let's pronounce the Ocean Spray medical clinic officially open.'

And to his astonishment it was fun. For every patient he saw Susie would fill him in on the history, tell him what she thought was wrong, let him know previous medications…She had comprehensive medical histories for everyone on the island filed in her head, as well as detailed notes.

'These are your patient files?' he asked in the gap in appointments she'd decreed necessary to fill him in on the next few patients.

'Yes.'

'The doctor has his own?'

'Not as comprehensive as mine. There's always something going wrong. I can second-guess most problems if I have a decent history.'

'So how do you cope with problems?'

'If they're haemorrhoids or similar, they see the mainland doctor when he comes over. If they have something like shingles, where early treatment is needed, then I make a tentative diagnosis, ring the doctor, have him agree with me and then the medication is sent over.'

'He always agrees with you?'

'Anything for a quiet life,' she said, wrinkling her nose. 'And he charges as if he's seen them.'

'So that's why you charge peanuts,' he said cautiously, looking at the desk where his last patient had set down a ten-dollar note before leaving. Ryan Flinders had just popped into the clinic to have his shingles checked. Susie had cleaned and dressed a raw patch of inflamed skin on his shoulder. Sam had checked his medication, had a look on the internet for current therapeutic guidelines and sent an urgent request to the pharmacy on the mainland to send a change of medication with the next supply boat.

Ten dollars?

'If you stayed here for a while you could be registered for government health rebates,' Susie said diffidently. 'You'd get paid well.'

'So what would I be paid for what we just did?'

'Long consultation. Dressing.' She gave him an amount and he nodded, thoughtful.

'That sounds reasonable. So how come you get ten dollars?'

'I'm not a doctor.'

'You're a very good nurse. Plus a great pilates teacher.'

She flushed, just a little. He liked it, he decided. She'd blush and she'd fight it. He'd watch while she tried to act nonchalant and he found it fascinating.

OK, he found her fascinating.

'Mr Flinders was a friend of my grandfather's.'

'You've just used five dollars' worth of dressings.'

'Yes, but—'

'How the hell are you making a living?'

'I'm fine,' she said and then added grudgingly, 'Your cheque will make a difference.'

'I'm dammed if I want Grant's cheque chewed up on dressings for the likes of Mr Flinders. I'm willing to bet he has more money than you do.'

'It's my lifestyle,' she said defensively. 'It's what I choose.'

'Do you like staying on this island?' he asked incredulously and she looked defensive.

'It's a great place to—'

'Raise kids or retire? What about practise medicine? Susie, you're a charity.'

'I'm not.'

'Every one of these people is a friend of your grandfather's. A friend of yours.'

'So?'

'So does the schoolteacher here work for peanuts because she knows everyone?'

'It's different. These people were good to me when—'

'When you came home with your babies. I'd imagine they were.' He softened. 'OK, Susie, I'll be nice to them, but I'm damned if I'm working for ten bucks an hour.'

'You're working for Effie visits.'

'No,' he said softly. 'I'm working for you.' He hesitated. She was looking confused. As well she might, he thought. He was feeling confused himself.

'I'm figuring out really fast that the Effie visits are a certainty,' he said softly. 'Could you refuse my Aunt Effie a visit to the twins? I don't think so. You're soft, Susie. No wonder Grant took advantage of you.'

'He didn't.'

'No?'

'I mean…'

'He used you,' he said softly. 'Everyone seems to be using you. Even this Brenda…'

'Oh, will you leave it?'

'She's your fifth cousin seven times removed and you support her.'

'She was housekeeper to Grandpa when I was away. I couldn't have left the island if she hadn't been here. And now she takes care of the twins.'

'She's a little…'

'Simple. Yes, she is,' Susie said defensively. 'She can't hold down a real job.'

'So you'll support her for ever.'

'And you'd have me throw her out. Like Grant.'

'I am not like Grant.' It came out of nowhere, a blast of icy anger so furious that it shocked them both. They were left staring warily at each other, wondering what had just happened.

'I'm sorry,' Sam said at last, and Susie attempted a smile.

'Does that mean I don't have to throw Brenda out to sleep under bridges?'

'There don't seem to be all that many bridges hereabouts to sleep under,' he said cautiously, and her smile firmed.

Great. He loved it when she smiled. But she was looking confused. That was what kept happening. He'd make her laugh and she'd relax, and then she'd think of Grant and haul herself back to reality. Which was confusing.

He had to figure out a way to find a new reality.

The door of the clinic opened and a young woman appeared, towing a child.

'Donna,' Susie said.

'Hi,' Donna said. 'Sorry, I'm not booked in but Thomas was trying to blow polystyrene balls out of his nostrils and one's gone down.' She looked hopefully at Sam. 'Susie tells me you have amazing ball skills.' She grinned.

Sam came as close to blushing as he'd ever come in his life. He took a step back and Donna chuckled.

'Sorry. Sorry. I couldn't resist it. This is all so perfect and far be it from me to mess it up with my innuendos. But Thomas really has got a ball stuck down there. Can you get it out, please?'

Sam loved it. A week went by and the fog in his head was almost a memory.

That his stay here had been extended indefinitely had been

accepted enthusiastically by every islander. They had a doctor on call, and symptoms were surfacing that had never seen the inside of a doctor's clinic before. They loved it that they could turn up at the tiny surgery set up next to the post office, sit on the post office steps and wait to see the doctor.

It wasn't an ideal surgery. It had originally been a first-aid post, a place where Susie could meet someone who needed stitches, who needed a bit of urgent attention while transfer was arranged to the mainland. It had a desk and two chairs and an examination couch, and the waiting room was the front steps. It was really squashed and he did think longingly about his magnificent office back home. But that was the only thing he missed.

He didn't have time to miss anything else.

He swam in Susie's cove every morning. That was compulsory—especially when on the second morning of his stay he'd gone down to the cove at dawn and discovered Susie was already there.

He'd seen she'd been disconcerted to have him join her. For a moment on that first morning she'd looked like she'd turn and go home.

'I'm sorry,' he'd said. 'There must be other swimming beaches nearer Doris's. I just didn't know them. I won't bother you again.'

'You're not bothering me,' she'd said, but he'd known that he was.

'I'll go.'

'No.' She shook her head. 'This is dumb. It's a big beach.'

She'd headed into the water with brisk determination. He'd followed, but that first morning he'd taken care not to swim anywhere near her.

On the third morning he was swimming across the cove, she was swimming in the other direction and suddenly she turned and started swimming beside him. They swam together for a bit, and then she pulled away. He pushed himself to keep up.

She pulled away again.

It became a challenge, one he suspected she was enjoying as much as he was. She swam for half an hour, seemingly unaware of him swimming beside her, but surely she must be as aware as he was. It was like there was some sixth sense— one he'd never known he'd had until now. The feeling that this woman was close by.

He could have swum for longer but Susie's swimming time was obviously restricted. Exactly half an hour after she'd entered the water she left, saying little, towelling herself dry then heading up the cliff to her car and going home, presumably to wake the twins up and start her day.

An hour later she'd phone him at Doris's and run through the patients who were booked to see him that morning. By the time he entered his clinic he had a comprehensive idea of what he was facing. One way or another, Susie's presence stayed with him all morning, be it as a memory of her acerbic patient commentaries—things like 'You'll be seeing Cheryl Barnes for her cough but she's smoking five packs a day. She'll lie through her teeth about it, but you might want to run it past her as a possible cause.' Or 'Leo Hasting's booked in because he's having trouble sleeping. His wife has early-stage Alzheimer's. There's a resource pamphlet in the desk drawer—I tried to give it to him last time he saw me but he refused. See if you can do any better.'

And in the quiet times between patients, there was the memory of her early-morning swimming.

He worked in his tiny surgery until lunchtime, while Susie ran her pilates classes. Then he walked back along the headland to have lunch with Doris. At two Susie collected him and they did house calls together.

And house calls with Susie were fun.

She was like a waft of a fresh sea breeze, he thought. She'd still be in the jogging suit she wore for pilates—'It's really comfy and it feels like a uniform,' she told him when he'd said it looked cute. It consisted of knee length joggers—bright yellow or bright red—a matching singlet and a tiny crimson or sea-green jacket. Her hair was always bunched in pigtails or braids, tied with a ribbon to match her joggers.

The islanders loved her. She breezed into their cottages and the islanders' pleasure was palpable. Even in the grimmest of circumstances they greeted her with smiles.

There were grim circumstances. This island had become almost a retirement home for elderly fisherfolk. The nearest nursing home was fifteen miles south on the mainland, Susie explained, and the Ocean Spray residents would rather die than go there.

'And that's not an exaggeration,' she explained as they finished a call that had left Sam almost speechless. Miriam Edwards was dying slowly of bone metastases. Her husband was caring for her with dogged pride and a level of exhaustion that seemed almost unbelievable.

'Miriam should be in a hospice,' Susie said. 'But it would mean Tom could only see her twice a week. She'd get much better pain control there—I'm really struggling to think of what I can do and get the doctors to agree to give me phone orders. Miriam is one of the reasons I agreed to this crazy contract. A doctor here, even if it's only for a week, is fantastic.'

'Thank you,' he said. But then he thought about it. 'No,' he said. 'There's no way I should be accepting compliments. What we're doing with Miriam is deeply satisfying.'

'You've given her her first pain-free sleep for a month,' she said. 'And Tom, too. I just wish so much I could get long-term help.'

'Once the bridge is rebuilt it'll be better,' he said, and she shrugged.

'If it's rebuilt. The powers that be are vacillating. And even when it's rebuilt, Doc Blaxson once a week if he can't think of an excuse is hardly good medical care. He's employed by the district hospital, and island medical care is part of his job description. But he does what he must and no more. He certainly doesn't care.' She eyed him with caution. 'Not like you do,' she said softly.

Sam didn't say anything. They drove to their next call without talking and he was grateful for her silence. He cared?

Yes, he thought. Amazingly, he did care, as he'd cared for little else for the last few months. He was falling in love with the medicine of this place. It was too small a population to ever make a living as a doctor—hell, Susan was struggling to make a living as a district nurse—but for the last few years, as he'd climbed the career ladder, he'd lost touch with this sort of medicine.

He was good at his job. Very good. The downside of that was that he was no longer the first point of contact for a patient. Well, he hadn't been that since his intern days, but as a junior orthopod he'd at least seen problems early. Now he was referred patients who were under the care of other specialists.

'Can you take a look at this hip?' the referral letter would say.

At this hip. Not at this person.

He wouldn't mind being able to do more than that again.

Thinking of that, though, had to wait until night-time, for after the house calls was his favourite time of the day.

'It's only because it's summer,' Susan told him. 'And because maybe I think it's important that the boys get to know their uncle.' But for whatever reason, she'd decided to let Sam in on her evening ritual.

They barbecued on the veranda and Sam was invited. Brenda was there, too, a quiet little woman with a head covered permanently in curlers—a woman waiting for ever for an excuse to take them off and party. But even when she went ballroom dancing her curlers stayed put, Susie told him, and he had the feeling they were part of her head.

Brenda was like a big kid. She was competent enough at the simple things—she'd be safe enough to leave in charge of the boys as necessity obviously decreed she must—but she'd hardly be good company for Susie. She giggled with the kids, she ate her sausages with gusto, she joined in their after-dinner game of beach cricket, then listened in on the twins' bedtime stories and retreated to watch television while Susie said goodbye to Sam.

On the first night Susie was inside before the first commercial break in Brenda's show.

On the second night it was the third commercial break before Sam left.

After that they gave up and Sam only left when they heard the end credits from Brenda's open window.

It was like releasing a pressure valve, Sam decided. He could talk to Susie as he'd never been able to talk to anyone. They steered away—by mutual unspoken consent—from the deeply personal. Like Grant. But there was so much that wasn't personal. They started off talking about shared patients. They ended up comparing star signs, discussing astrology and then astronomy, favourite car colours, soccer teams, the virtues of wool socks over synthetic, favourite Beatle—deep divide over that—predilection for oatmeal over cereal, anything and everything, closer and closer...

And on the sixth night they kissed.

It wasn't meant to happen. Or at least maybe Susie hadn't meant it to happen. In truth, Sam had been thinking of very little else. He knew it was dumb. Grant had hurt Susie so badly that to try and kindle any sort of passion must end in disaster.

But she was irresistible. She was different to any woman he'd ever met, and on that sixth night, when the end credits started and he'd risen out of the swing to take his leave, he tugged her up to join him, and instead of holding her steady at arm's length, suddenly she was in his arms.

She was lovely.

She'd changed out of her normal island gear—the gym outfit that was her standard work uniform—at night. She was wearing a faded pair of denim shorts and a frayed white T-shirt. She'd tugged the ribbon from her braid so it was unadorned, and she'd been playing beach cricket in bare feet. The moon was rising behind her, and she was so lovely that she took his breath away. So what was a man to do? He'd have had to be inhuman to resist.

He kissed her softly, hesitantly, on the top of her head, half expecting her to react with anger. But she didn't pull away. Amazingly her hands came up to hold him, tugging gently at his hips to bring him forward and bridge the gap between them.

She turned her face up to his. For a long moment he stared down at her in the moonlight, and then, gently, wondrously, he lowered his face and he kissed her as he had wanted to kiss her since they'd met.

And just like that, his universe shifted, realigned, settled. It was like some giant jumble of jigsaw pieces falling gently into place. His world had been out of kilter, off true. Now it settled where it ought to be.

Susie.

How the hell could he ever have thought he could marry Marilyn? he thought wildly. And how could Grant possibly not have wanted to marry Susie?

Her lips were softly yielding, yet her hands were on his hips, tugging him forward, holding him against her as if she was doing a claiming of her own. Their kiss deepened and deepened again. She tasted of the sea. Of the last vestiges of barbecue. Of Susie.

How long it lasted he could never afterwards remember. All he knew was that this was timeless. It was a full stop, let's pause and regroup and start again, with things as they were meant to be.

She was meant to be here.

His hands were holding her tight against him. Her T-shirt was skimpy and his hands naturally ended up on the exposed skin of her waist. She was warm and smooth and infinitely inviting.

He shifted back, just slightly, to see. 'Susie…'

'Don't stop.'

'Yeah, stop.'

The intruding voice broke in with a jolt. Her television show was over, and now Brenda had stuck her head out the window to see where Susie was. Now she was gazing at them both in affronted amazement.

'Susan, don't let him do that.'

They pulled apart, and it seemed as if Susie was as reluctant as he was.

'Why not?' Susie asked, her voice a husky whisper.

'He's a man,' Brenda said.

'Oh,' Susie said, looking up at him in the moonlight. 'So he is.'

'I'm making cocoa,' Brenda said. 'Tell him to go home so we can have cocoa and go to bed.'

'Go home, Sam,' Susie said, but her eyes weren't saying go home at all. She smiled up at him, a trifle rueful. 'OK, then. Maybe you'd better. Go home so we can make cocoa and go to bed.'

'Yes, ma'am,' he said. But he was still holding her and she wasn't making the slightest effort to pull away. 'I'd hate to keep you from your cocoa. Same time, same place tomorrow?'

'Sounds good.'

'It sounds really good,' he said softly, and he tugged her forward and kissed her lightly on the lips, one more time, just because he had to, and then he let her go, turned and disappeared into the night.

* * *

'Why did you let him kiss you?' Once he'd gone Brenda was venting her outrage, acting as if she'd personally been violated. 'You can't just…let him.'

'I guess that's exactly what I did.' Susie was sitting at the kitchen table with her mug of cocoa, starting dreamily into the middle distance.

'You're not going to marry him, are you?'

Her happy little haze dissipated, just like that. 'I… No,' she whispered.

'Then don't let him kiss you.'

'Maybe I shouldn't.'

'You know you shouldn't. Anyway,' Brenda grumbled, carrying her mug across to the sink and dumping it on the draining-board with a savage little thump, 'he's from America. Even if you wanted to marry him you couldn't. We need you here.'

'I know that.' She hadn't meant her tone to be so sharp. She swallowed and tried again. 'It's OK, Brenda. I just kissed him.'

'Then don't do it again,' Brenda said crossly. 'I don't like it.'

'He's a nice man.'

'Yes, but I want things to stay the same,' Brenda said. 'That's what we all want.'

'Things do change, though,' Susie said doubtfully. 'Like the bridge falling down. That's different.'

'It's not,' Brenda said, suddenly triumphantly sure of her ground. 'Cos there wasn't a bridge here for ages and your dad was the ferryman. Then there was a bridge and now look at it. We're back to where we started. No bridge.' She wrinkled her nose, clearly thinking deeply. 'Hey, I know,' she said at last. 'Maybe you can kiss him. Maybe you could marry him and buy a new ferryboat and Sam could be the new ferryman. The twins would like that.'

'No,' said Susie.

'No?'

'No.'

Brenda glowered, unwilling to lose such a neat plan.

'If you don't want him to be our new ferryman then don't kiss him,' she ordered. 'Leave him alone.'

Susie stared into the dregs of her cocoa. Brenda waited for her to agree.

But Susie was saying nothing.

'You kissed Susie last night.'

It was seven-thirty and Doris was pouring Sam's breakfast coffee and her tone was accusatory. Sam almost dropped his cup.

'How the hell—?'

'Nothing happens on this island without everyone else finding out half an hour ago,' Doris told him. She set down her coffee-pot and fixed Sam with a look that said she was fifty years older than he was and she intended to speak her mind. 'Don't you mess her about.'

'I wouldn't.'

'Your brother did.'

'How—'

'I told you. The place is bugged. And you're his twin. You mess Susie around and you'll be tarred and feathered and run out of town on a rail.'

'Or on a boat,' he said, but she didn't smile.

'I'm serious, Sam.'

'I think I am, too,' he told her.

There was a moment's loaded silence. 'You mean it?' Doris said at last, and Sam shook his head.

'I don't know. It's way too early. But she's a great woman.'

'We need her,' Doris said flatly, and then, as Sam frowned, she winced and continued.

'It's not fair,' she said. 'I'd be the first to say it's not fair. But if you wanted to whisk her off to the US to give her a happy ever after, we'd be in one hell of a mess. She wouldn't leave the twins. She wouldn't leave Brenda and she wouldn't leave us.'

'I'm not asking her to.'

'But you kissed her.'

'Yes. But…'

'But it's just a holiday romance?'

'I don't know,' he said helplessly, and she nodded.

'Maybe you don't,' she said. 'Sam, what you've been doing here is terrific. I'm thinking I might even give you a cut in your room rate. But not if you're messing with Susie. How long are you staying?'

'I'm not sure,' he said. 'Until my great-aunt comes.'

'Which is when?'

'A few days?'

'And that's all.'

'I'm not—'

'That wasn't a question,' Doris said flatly. 'It's an order. Three days after your great-aunt arrives I cross off your booking. We love having a doctor here but not if it means you're making Susie unhappy.'

'I'm not making Susie unhappy.'

'You will,' she said darkly. 'And that's not a question either.'

'Susie, he's gorgeous.'

'He is, isn't he?' Come hell or high water, pilates classes went on. Donna hadn't been able to catch Susie all week, and in desperation had booked into her class. Susie had her balanced on the reformer bench, doing cat stretches against counterweights. She thought that might shut her friend up, but no such luck.

'So you're seeing him again tonight?'

'I might be.'

'And you're serious?'

'Of course she's serious.' Perched on the saddle of the exercise bike, pedalling gamely, Muriel was ready to proffer an opinion on everyone. 'He's the first good-looking young man to appear on the island for ten years. Excepting your Nick,' she conceded to Donna. 'And you had to drag Nick here against his will.'

'I merely bore him children who he adored, got him addicted to my cooking and then said I was coming home,' Donna said. 'That's not dragging.'

'It's almost dragging,' Doris retorted, wrinkling her brow as she concentrated on getting her legs higher. 'And you had to go off the island to find someone. Our Susan can't do that.'

'She did do that,' Donna retorted. 'She found Sam in London.'

'No,' Doris said. 'She found Grant. The twins' father.'

'Same thing,' Donna said. 'Identical twins.'

'They're not the same,' Susie snapped.

'Would you have fallen for him if he didn't look like Grant?' Donna asked.

'No.' She swallowed and regrouped. 'That is…I haven't fallen for him.'

'Pull the other leg,' Donna said. 'You're glowing. You're head over heels in love.'

'But you can't leave,' Muriel said anxiously.

'Then she'll just have to do what I did with my Nick,' Donna said. 'Blackmail him…I mean, coerce him gently into seeing what's good for him.'

'He's a specialist,' Doris retorted. 'He's an orthopaedic surgeon. He couldn't make a living on this island. The council's saying now they mightn't even have the money to rebuild the bridge. How could we cope without Susie?'

'We'd survive,' Donna said stoutly—but she sounded unsure.

'Of course you would.' Finally Susie managed to get a word in. 'You might have to because if you start organising my love life any more I might leave in a huff and you'll never see me again.'

'You couldn't leave us,' Doris said.

'You couldn't leave Brenda,' Muriel added.

Donna looked doubtfully at her friend. 'She might have to,' she said softly. 'Susie, you need to do what you need to do.'

'Well, I would,' Susie retorted, really flustered. 'If I had to leave the island then, of course, I would. But I don't need to. You're all talking nonsense. Just because I'm enjoying myself a little…'

'You're falling in love,' Donna said.

'I'm not,' she said stoutly. 'To fall in love is ridiculous. Yes, he's a personable guy. He's a skilled doctor and that's great. He's the twins' uncle and I need to be nice to him. And I don't mind admitting that…that…'

'Don't say any more,' Donna begged. 'At least…not to everyone. Just to me.'

'She can talk to us,' Doris said, offended. 'We're family.'

'The whole island's family,' Muriel retorted. 'That's the problem.' She brightened. 'Maybe we could make Dr Sam one of us. An honorary islander.'

'And have him taking half the responsibility for pilates?' Donna demanded. 'Or have him practise medicine with a patient base of five hundred and no hospital?'

'It does sound a bit rough,' Doris said. 'He could do it as a retirement job but he's hardly ready for retirement.'

'He's not, is he?' Susie said, struggling to keep her voice even. 'Neither is he in the least interested in any sort of job here. So butt out everyone. This is my business, and no one else's. I was dumb to even start it. I was dumb to think that I could possibly have a bit of fun without the whole island taking over and making a haystack out of a needle or whatever stupid analogy I'm trying to think up. And pilates is over as of now, because I have to go and take a cold shower before I hit someone. Before I hit three someones in particular. Doris, I refuse to take you out of the trapeze. May you hang there until your legs drop off.' She leaned over the control panel of

Muriel's exercise bike and moved the dial to 'Mountain—Extreme'. And she stalked over to Donna's reformer and heaved another four springs onto the counterweight.

'There,' she snapped. 'You've all just graduated. I'm out of here. You don't need me at all.'

She stalked out of the room and slammed the door after her. She leaned heavily on the door and counted to ten.

She went back in.

They were exactly as she'd left them, staring at the doorway in consternation.

'I would have got us all off,' Donna said.

'Sure you would,' Susie said wearily, and lifted the weights free. 'You could all get by just fine without me. As I can get by fine without Sam. The thing is that you don't have to prove it.'

CHAPTER NINE

SHE couldn't take a cold shower.

She went through the remainder of exercises with her group of three. She bade them goodbye. Donna wanted to stay, looking desperate for a talk, but Susie was having none of it.

Donna was a part of the problem, she thought. When Donna had made her decision in Port Lincoln to come back here, would she have come if she hadn't been here? No, Susie decided. As well as Susie's friendship, Donna also needed some sort of medical security for her large family.

So she was part of the trap.

'But it's not a trap,' she said to herself as she closed the door on the last of them. They were assuming something that wasn't happening. They were assuming she was attracted to Sam.

Yeah, OK, that wasn't such a baseless assumption, she admitted. She was head over heels attracted to Sam. But that didn't mean she'd lose her head and fall for him the same stupid way she'd fallen for his brother. She was simply enjoying his company while he was here. Soon he'd be gone and she'd be left with…with…

With her kids, with Brenda, with her friends, her work, her island. Not such a bad deal. She didn't need Sam.

But she'd see him tonight. She'd promised to take him

prawning. That was good. Activity rather than talk. Talk was dangerous. Getting to know him was dangerous.

It was for such a short time. Surely it couldn't hurt to let her defences down a little…

Her phone went. She flipped it open, then tried to suppress a little fillip of pleasure when Sam's name came up on the screen.

'Hi,' she said, and then made it more formal. 'Good morning. Can I help you?'

'I've got an ingrown toenail,' he said, and she heard him smile.

'I'm sorry to hear it,' she said cautiously. 'Does it need urgent air evacuation to the mainland?'

He chuckled. She liked his chuckle.

'Nope.'

'It can't be very ingrown,' she said. 'You were walking OK last night.'

'It's not my toe.'

'But it's your toenail?' Drat being formal. She was smiling with him, thinking he shared her sense of the ridiculous. She liked it that she could make him chuckle, and she loved it that he made her smile right back.

'It's Dottie Carmichael's toenail.'

'And Dottie Carmichael's toe?'

'You have it in one, Einstein,' he said, and she could still hear him smile. 'But she's pretty anxious about exposing her private parts to a male doctor.'

'Her private parts being her toe?'

'That's the one.'

'Tell her I'll see her tomorrow,' she said.

'The pain's unbearable, Doc,' Sam said, and Susie heard Dottie's querulous tone mimicked to a nicety. 'I dunno when I've been more relieved than when I thought, Thank God, we have two medics on the island—one can be anaesthetist and one can be surgeon.'

'You're kidding.'

'Nope,' Sam said. 'She's sitting on our waiting steps with her foot swathed in a bandage so big I thought at the very least she had a balloon-sized lymphoedema. But no. Just one slightly pinkish toe. She's waiting for you to hotfoot it over here and put her out of her misery.'

'I'm in the middle of pilates.'

'You're at the end of your pilates,' Sam said patiently. 'Dottie told me. You have three one-hour sessions every Tuesday morning, you finish at twelve so at twelve-twenty—which would be in about ten minutes—you're free for lifesaving surgery.'

'Says Dottie?'

'Says Dottie. Does this island run every minute of your life?'

'Yes,' she said, and she sighed. 'It does.'

'I'll tell her to come back tomorrow.'

'No,' she said. 'I may as well come now.'

'Do the twins come home for lunch?'

'No.'

'Then we could have a sandwich on the beach after our life-saving surgery.'

'I don't know whether that's wise.'

'It might take too long,' Sam said, ready to agree. 'We'll schedule two hours but there's recovery time as well, and then there's counselling of traumatised relatives. Maybe we'd better make it dinner.'

'Maybe we'd better make it neither.'

He heard it then. The smile in his voice faded. 'Is there something wrong?'

'No. I…'

'Of course I can put Dottie off.'

'I may as well do it now.'

'Then what's bothering you?'

'Just… Nothing,' she said. 'Nothing at all. Sorry, Sam, I've just had a big morning.'

'Did something happen at Pilates?' It was a serious question. He somehow knew her, she thought. She didn't know how, but somehow he saw inside her, in a way no one else ever had. Certainly not Grant. More and more she thought that comparing them was unfair. They were two different people. Sam made her smile, and he watched her smile and it gave him pleasure.

Well, making him smile gave her pleasure as well. Damn the islanders, she thought. They had no business unsettling her. Sam was nice and he was a friend and he was the twins' uncle. He'd be gone in a week or less. So, dammit, she was going to enjoy it now.

'I'm being dumb,' she said, forcing herself to sound bright and chirpy. 'I'll be right over. You get the surgery ready. Do you think we should call for a few blood donors in case we run short?'

'If we have you, then Dottie and I need nothing else,' Sam said softly, and he ended the call before she could respond.

She should go straight over. But instead she sat on the seat outside her pilates clinic and watched the sea for a minute.

'If we have you, we need nothing else.'

The smile had gone from his voice. She'd heard his tone change.

He was serious.

Nonsense, she told herself bracingly. Nonsense, nonsense, nonsense.

A week and nothing more. Get on with it.

Dottie's ingrown toenail awaited.

'When's Effie coming?'

They'd finished their lifesaving surgery. They'd done a

house call together. Then they'd bought sandwiches at the general store and ice creams. They were now sitting on what was left of the bridge, dangling their legs over the edge and watching the tide swirl in underneath them.

She felt like a kid on holiday. The sun was warm on her shoulders. The ice cream was great. Sam was sitting beside her, loose-limbed, relaxed, carefree. Feeding crumbs from his cone to the minnows below.

'Friday,' he said, and she had to think about what she'd asked. Effie was coming on Friday. Great. Or was it?

'How long do you think she'll stay?' she asked.

'Doris has us both booked in for three days. That means we leave on Monday.'

'Oh.'

They concentrated on their ice creams for a bit.

'How much did Grant hurt you?' he asked, casually, as if it didn't matter too much if she didn't want to answer. 'I mean…I know he left you pregnant, but…were you really in love with him?'

'I was pretty young,' she said diffidently.

'That means he hurt you a lot.'

'I was pretty dumb.'

'There's a difference between dumb and innocent.'

'Grant was young, too.'

'Grant would have been twenty-eight. What were you? Twenty-one?'

'I… Yes.'

'And you promised to marry him?'

'Like I said, I was dumb.'

'I'm so sorry.'

'There's no need for you to be sorry,' she said, with asperity. 'You're not responsible for your brother.'

'No, but he's messing with my future.'

'How?'

'I'm falling in love with you,' he said softly, and the world stilled.

'No,' she said at last. 'You can't.'

'Why can't I?'

'Because…'

'Of Grant?'

'Yes,' she said helplessly. 'No. For all sorts of reasons. I can't even begin to explain.'

'If I found a way through all those reasons,' he said softly, feeding more of his cone to the shoal of waiting fish, 'would you think that maybe I just might?'

'You just might…what?'

'Fall in love with you.'

'Grant told me he was in love with me.'

'Grant was a liar.'

'He was your brother.'

'He was a liar,' Sam said heavily. 'He lived for nothing but himself. You know, ever since he died I've been feeling…desolate. I've been trying to figure it out. I see my patients, often elderly people at the end of their lives, but sometimes younger ones, kids with carcinomas, ghastly stuff. And I get emotionally involved and I feel sick when they die. But with Grant…'

He hesitated. 'I've figured it out. I spent sessions with a shrink trying to sort it and I couldn't—I've been thick with depression and I didn't know why. But here…I've suddenly seen it. Grant's life was an absolute waste. It wasn't that his death was a tragedy—maybe I could have dealt with that more easily. But from the time he was born he thought of nothing but himself. He lied and he cheated and he trampled on people. It was all such a stupid, stupid waste. So I haven't been grieving that he's dead. I've been grieving that he never lived.'

'Sam…'

'I bet he never fed fish ice-cream cone,' he said, and broke off another piece. And another. And then… Catastrophe. The remainder of his cone cracked. His hardly eaten double scoop of chocolate ice cream slipped through the remainder of his cone and fell into the water. The minnows bolted in panic and the blob of chocolate sank slowly to the bottom.

'Aargh,' Sam said.

'You can share mine,' Susie said.

He looked at her with adoration. 'I love you,' Sam said.

'You don't know me,' Susie whispered.

'I know you like blueberry ice cream when the only decent ice cream in the whole world is chocolate,' Sam said. 'Yet still I love you.'

'Sam, be serious.'

'I've lost my ice cream. It's very serious.'

'Don't,' she said sharply, and he turned to her and smiled, a gentle, heart-warming smile that made her world stand still.

'Don't?'

'Don't tease.'

'I'm not teasing.'

'Grant asked me to marry him,' she said flatly, and watched his face still.

'But he didn't mean it,' he said at last. 'And I'm not Grant. Neither am I asking you to marry me. There's a whole lot of complicating factors at play here. A major one being this bridge. What do you think our chances are of getting the entire island to evacuate to the mainland?'

'Somewhere between zero and Buckley's.'

'Buckley's?'

'Buckley was a convict early in Australia's European settlement. He escaped for over thirty years but still ended up captured.' Yeah, OK she was rabbiting on, but she was relieved to be on safer ground. 'And Buckley and Nunn was a well-known department store in Melbourne. So when things are hopeless we say we've got Buckley's chance. Or Nunn.'

'I see,' he said cautiously, and she giggled, despite her discomfort, at the ludicrous look of bemusement on his face.

'You'll have to stay a lot longer than a week to learn Australian,' she told him.

'I wouldn't mind staying,' he said.

Her ground was suddenly really, really shaky again. 'Sam, I can't,' she said, panicked. 'I mean…'

'I know you can't,' he said. 'So all I'm saying now is that I've fallen for you. I know it's a disaster that I'm Grant's twin. I know that makes it almost impossible for you. I know also that it's a mess that this island is dependent on you. That makes it almost impossible as well. And the twins and Brenda…This Buckley?' he asked cautiously. 'Did he end up hanged?'

'I don't think he did,' Susie said, confused. 'He lived with the native Australians for thirty years and then did a nice line in a lecture tour.'

'There you are, then,' he said. 'So Buckley's isn't impossible.'

'Sam…'

'The only thing that would make it impossible is if you look at me now and say, "Sam, don't take this one step further. Don't even think about loving me because I can't ever love you back. Never." Can you say that, Susie?'

'I don't…'

'Neither can I,' he said, and he carefully removed her ice cream from her hands, licked its drips from the edges, leaned forward, kissed her on the nose and handed it back.

'I haven't got a clue. But even if you like blueberry and not chocolate, I think we ought to work on it together.'

'But I can't…'

'Love me?'

'I don't know,' she whispered, and then her phone rang and she swore. 'I haven't got time. I can't think.'

'And I'll not be rushing you,' he said, and he lifted the phone from her top pocket and answered it.

'Ocean Spray Medical Service?'

He listened intently. 'Really? Goodness me. What a catastrophe. No, you just lie down very, very quietly and wait for help. The entire medical contingent of Ocean Spray is on its way. Just as soon as we finish our ice cream.'

He flipped the phone closed and popped it back into her pocket. 'I don't mean to hurry you,' he said, 'but we have an emergency.'

'I… What?'

'You know we told Dottie to go home and put her feet up?'

'I… Yes.'

'It seems she decided to feed the chooks first. Chooks. Do I have that right? That'd be poultry, I'm guessing.'

'Poultry,' she said, deciding to join in. 'That's a bit of a toffy name for chooks.'

'Chooks,' he said again, sounding the name with satisfaction. 'I'm a fast learner. Anyway, Dottie's spilt the chooks' dinner over her bandage and it's soggy and she's sitting on the back step, waiting for us to hotfoot it over there.'

'Gee,' Susie said, trying not to grin. 'Just as well we have a trained US orthopaedic surgeon to hand.'

'Years and years of training,' he said, rising and putting out a hand to help her rise with him. 'Come to this. The culmination of a great and glorious career.'

She shouldn't take his hand. She shouldn't go one step further with this lovely, gentle, laughing man who was the echo of what had almost destroyed her once before.

But he was waiting for her to put her hand in his. He was smiling down at her, laughing with his eyes, and there was no choice at all.

He tugged her to her feet and he kissed her. The kiss deepened and it didn't matter at all that they were standing on the bridge and anyone on shore could see them. It didn't matter at all that she was kissing him back, taking as well as giving, feeling that her world was righting itself somehow, that miracles could happen, that a happy ending wasn't just for fairy-tales.

It didn't matter at all that her ice cream slipped sideways and then fell, a mound of blueberry ice cream dropping to sit by the chocolate on the riverbed, and her cone disintegrating to make a thousand minnows below them delirious with delight.

Second time around and maybe it was the right time. Maybe…just maybe…

CHAPTER TEN

HE HAD to figure it out.

Effie was coming on Friday. Doris was adamant about her three day rule and there was nowhere else to stay on the island. So he had to get it sorted before she came.

Susie was trapped. He had to get her untrapped. But to take her off the island…

He couldn't do it. Neither did he want to. He spent each evening with Joel and Robbie, and the little boys crept into his heart with almost ludicrous ease. Sure, they were family. Their resemblance to him was uncanny. But it wasn't just that.

He'd never had much to do with children. He had no extended family—cousins, nieces, nephews. His specialty was adult orthopaedics so even in his work he seldom met kids.

He and Marilyn had discussed—in theory—the possibility of a family, but to Marilyn it had been a remote possibility, something that might happen if there was a chance she could take a few months off from her career. Sam had always thought he didn't much care either way.

But now…these little boys had blasted into his life with energy and enthusiasm and a joy that blew him out of his indifference.

The night after he'd kissed Susie on the bridge he was reading them a bedtime story while Susie folded washing—

yeah, corny and domestic, but for someone with his background it was more joyous than being given a free feed in a Michelin-rated restaurant. Joel was bouncing and bubbly, but Robbie was quiet.

'Is something wrong?' he asked gently as he tucked the little boy in, and Robbie looked up at Sam and sniffed. Manfully. Trying not to cry.

'My volcano won't spurt,' he confessed.

On closer investigation it seemed the boys were involved in science projects for school. Joel was making a marble race—exciting and successful. Robbie had made a plaster-of-Paris volcano, and he thought he'd be able to tuck a box of matches inside, drop a lighted match and watch it spurt.

It hadn't worked, and where Joel would have told the world his problems, Robbie was silently despondent. His despair and his silence hit a nerve within Sam, echoing his own childhood.

So two a.m. saw him sitting up in Doris's attic, playing with matches. The next night—after extensive reading, a bit of blind luck and a practice in Doris's kitchen—their nightly beach cricket match was replaced by lava-creating. While Susie and Joel watched, entranced, he and Robbie lined Robbie's scooped-out crater with plastic, then filled it with warm water thickened with flour and a generous dollop of red food colouring. When it came time for the volcano to erupt, he helped Robbie mix a little water with bicarbonate of soda. Robbie inserted it via a medical syringe—filched from a bemused Susie's medical bag—and then gave the volcano a gentle shake.

The result was truly spectacular. Robbie whooped with joy, Susie and Joel and Brenda cheered, and Sam thought it felt great to make this tiny family happy.

More. It made him happy. Even the scary Brenda was getting under his skin, demanding her own turn at lava-making. And Susie was glowing.

He loved Susie glowing. He just loved Susie. And he loved the kids. Dammit, any minute now he'd decide he loved Brenda. He had it bad.

He wouldn't leave them. More and more he realised that he couldn't. And to ask them to leave the island was equally impossible.

On Wednesday he asked Nick to take him across to the mainland.

'Getting claustrophobic on the island?' Nick teased as they made the crossing. Donna's husband was a big, silent fisherman who was starting to seem a friend. Hell, Sam thought as he stood by the wheel of Nick's boat and headed across the river. The whole island was starting to seem like friends.

'I can't see myself bandaging Dottie's toes for the rest of my life, if that's what you mean,' he told Nick, half joking, but Nick didn't smile in response.

'That's what our Susie does.'

'I know.'

'She's never had a chance to do much else.'

'Do you seriously think she'd leave?' Sam asked, and Nick thought about it and shook his head.

'Nah. She's got too much conscience. But Donna says she's going to break her heart over you.'

'She's not,' Sam said shortly, and that was that until they reached the jetty on the mainland. Sam had pre-ordered a taxi, and the driver was already waiting for him.

'Donna knows Susie real well,' Nick said as he held the boat steady while Sam climbed off. He sounded unhappy. 'Sam, you're a mate, but to mess with her…'

'I'm not.'

'Maybe you already have,' Nick said bluntly. 'So what're you doing today?'

'I'm buying some clothes for a start,' Sam said. 'I need to sort out the insurance on the car. And a few other things.'

'You mean fixing flights out of here?'

'I'm not sure,' Sam said. 'Maybe not yet.'

'Doris only has you booked until next Monday.'

'Yeah,' Sam said. 'So I have to work fast.'

One day without Sam and her world was empty. He'd said he had things to do on the mainland and of course he did. He didn't have clothes, a car, his paperwork, everything had sunk with the bridge, and of course he'd have to get it sorted. But his little clinic was closed and it wasn't just Susie who missed him.

'I had a toe check-up this morning,' Dottie told her, incensed that she'd left her chooks and come into town for nothing.

'I can check your toe.'

'You're not the same as Dr Sam.'

'I'm better than nothing,' Susie said, trying to sound positive, but Dottie shook her head.

'No, dear, you're not, and maybe that's what the problem is. Maybe the government doesn't think they have to provide a doctor because you're here.'

'You're thinking if I leave they might send a doctor?' Susie asked, bemused.

'Sam likes it here,' Dottie said. 'Only last night I was telling him the best spot to fish for mulloway. They don't run for another couple of months and I told him that, but he still wanted to know where to fish for them. So I reckon he might stay.'

'If I left.'

'Doris says he's sweet on you,' Dottie said. 'But you've got the littlies and he's a single man who could have anyone. What we need is for him to meet a nice young local girl with no ties. Then you could go back to the city.'

'He's gone to the mainland today,' Susie said shortly, trying

not to sound grumpy—but not succeeding. A sense of humour
could only go so far.

'Well, he'll have to go into the police station—the police
said they wanted him to file a report. Bethany's the receptionist there and she's a taking little thing.'

'So he'll bring back a bride tonight and I can leave tomorrow.'

'Now you've taken offence,' Dottie said, not perturbed in
the least. 'It's not that we don't appreciate you, dear, we do—
very much. It's just…Dr Sam's really special. And I say things
as I see them.'

'Sit down and let me take off your bandage,' Susie said
shortly. 'He might be special but until he comes home bearing
a bride, you're stuck with me.'

Sam didn't return that night. He texted her on his cellphone.
'There's official stuff I have to cope with. I need to take a quick
trip to Melbourne.'

She shouldn't be disappointed.

She was.

Beach cricket wasn't the same. Robbie and Joel had got
their marks for their science projects and Robbie had topped
the class. Even Joel was happy for him, and they both wanted
to tell Sam.

They could ring him, Susie thought, but then…but then…

She didn't ring. She put the twins to bed early and then
caught up on a mound of medical paperwork that had built up
because every night since he'd been there she'd spent with Sam.

She went to bed that night and stared at the ceiling, aching
for Sam.

'Which is just dumb. I haven't even slept with him.'

'He hasn't even asked you to sleep with him.'

'That's good. He's not Grant.'

The conversation with herself was getting her nowhere. She

got up and walked out onto the veranda to stare across at the distant mainland.

Where was he?

He could walk away now and never come back, she thought. He was a free agent. She might never see him again.

The thought was dreadful.

'Grant left me,' she told the sea.

'Grant promised you the world and then left you. Sam's promised you nothing.'

Strangely, that made her feel better. She sat on the swing for a while and things settled. Sam's smile was still with her. His gentle chuckle. The way he played with the boys, respectful of their needs, treating them as equals, sensing intuitively the boundaries he shouldn't cross.

'He's wonderful,' she whispered into the night.

'Yeah, and you're a moron,' she answered herself. 'You're sitting out here when you ought to be asleep. If you're going to stay awake then go do some more medico-legal stuff for the repat people. And stop thinking about Sam.'

As if.

She went back to her desk to work.

Sam stayed with her every word she wrote.

His last stop before leaving Melbourne was at a jeweller's. Not just any jeweller's, but one Carly Hammond recommended.

In the burns unit at South General, Pete was recovering well, but his wife was hardly leaving his side. Sam looked at Carly's rings and realised she was the lady to ask.

'Hell, we owe you so much. Can we buy something for you?' Pete asked, but Sam shook his head.

'Thanks, but, no, thanks,' he said. 'This is one purchase a man should make on his own.'

'Oh,' Carly said, and her eyes misted over. 'To Susan?'

She'd heard all about the rescue by now and her gratitude was endless.

'If she'll have me,' he said simply.

'She must,' Pete said, holding Carly's hand and tugging her close. 'A loving marriage…there's nothing in the world better than that. Even dumb boats…I bought that thing and thought I was the king of the world until I underestimated its acceleration and nearly killed myself. Now it's a heap of charred metal and I couldn't care less. Carly here is what's important. So you go to it, boy, but let us know where and let us know when. I'm going to be off crutches at your wedding if it kills me.'

So all he had to do was ask her.

Effie would be here in the morning. He should stay on the mainland for another night and wait for her but, hell, some questions just had to be asked right now.

Nick was picking him up at the wharf. Then there'd be four more hours until the twins went to bed, and even then there might be medical emergencies.

'The advice will be two aspirins and a good lie-down for anything from cholera to snakebite on the island tonight,' he told himself. 'Tonight just might…happen.'

CHAPTER ELEVEN

PROPOSING to Marilyn had been simple. He'd been able to organise rosters so they were both solidly off call. Then he'd contacted one of the country's best restaurants and organised a private booth. It had been easy, even if it hadn't felt absolutely right.

But that had been Marilyn. This was Susie. This proposal— or intended proposal—did feel absolutely right, but the ring was burning a hole in his pocket, and private booths were hard to find.

When they tied up at the wharf Susie was waiting for him and her mind wasn't on romance.

'I'm glad you're back. Elsie Barr's got a really bad stomach upset,' she told him. 'I'm worried that it might be appendicitis. Nick, can you not tie up for the night until we're sure? We might have to get you to take her back to the mainland. Sam, can you come and see?'

It was indeed appendicitis. Elsie was relatively young for the island—mid-sixties—but she looked older. She was pale and sweaty, her pulse was racing, and when Sam probed her tummy and then released the pressure she moaned.

'Rebound,' he said softly to Susie, and she nodded.

'That's what I thought. I wanted Nick to take her over to the mainland when he went to get you but she wouldn't go.'

'I don't want to go,' Elsie said helplessly. 'Who'll take care of my cats?'

'My boys and I will,' Susie said, with no hesitation. 'Elsie, you need to have that appendix out.'

'I can't,' she said, tearful. 'Susie, I won't.'

'There's nothing to be frightened of, Mrs Barr,' Sam said, taking her hand. 'We just need to cut a tiny slit into your tummy while you're under anaesthetic, take out your appendix, mop up what's left, give you a bit of antibiotic and then bring you home again.'

'We?' Elsie said, suspicious.

'I mean, the doctors on the mainland.'

'You said we,' Elsie said.

'Of course he said we,' Susie said from behind him. 'This is Sam, island doctor, at least till his aunty comes to take him home. There you go, Sam. You and Elsie pop across to the mainland and bring her appendix home in a jar.'

'A jar,' Sam said faintly, and she grinned.

'I knew you'd agree. I'll just tell Nick you're coming and find you a nice clean jam jar.'

So with the ring still in his pocket he went back to the mainland. The ambulance met them at the dock, but Elsie clung on and Sam just knew Susie would expect him to stay until the operation was over. So stay he did.

'But don't you dare go back without me,' he told Nick.

'How long do appendicectomies take?' Nick demanded, startled.

'Seconds,' Sam lied. 'We'll pop Elsie to sleep and next thing you know Elsie's appendix and I will be back here, waiting to return.'

With the box in my pocket, he thought.

* * *

It was eight o'clock. With Nick and Sam both away on medical business it seemed a good excuse for Donna and Susie and the kids to have dinner together. Susie and Donna were now supervising a game of Scrabble in Mrs Barr's living room. Kids and cats were everywhere, but the kids were starting to tire.

'They should be back any minute now,' Susie said cheerfully, emerging from the kitchen with cocoa for all. 'I just rang the hospital. It seems the anaesthetist's home in bed with flu so the surgeon asked Sam to gas for him. Joe, the surgeon, seems to think Sam's anaesthetist credentials are OK.' She flushed faintly and then grinned and added, 'As well as everything else about him.'

Why had she said that? It had come from nowhere and the kids' chatter died, giving the words emphasis. As Donna's eyebrows hiked, she went on hurriedly, 'The operation went fine.' She put down the cocoa tray a bit too hard and concentrated on mopping up splashes. 'Nick and Sam are on their way home. But there's no need for you to stay. The kids and I are fine here. We brought our sleeping bags. Nick can drop Sam at Doris's on the way back to your place.'

'If they're on their way, I may as well wait,' Donna said diffidently, her eyebrows remaining hiked. 'Nick texted me to say he's coming via here.'

'Why?'

'He seems to think Sam wants to see you tonight.'

'Sam can see me in the morning.'

'Nick says he needs to see you tonight.'

'Has he said he does?'

'I don't know. But Nick thinks he does, so Nick needs to bring him here, though why you're babysitting six cats…'

'Come on, Donna, what choice do I have?'

'Lots of choices,' Donna said obliquely. 'Lots and lots. According to my Nick, and he's a fisherman.'

'What's that got to do with—'

'Nick can track changes in the wind,' Donna said wisely, and then grinned and stood up, setting her cocoa aside and lifting the baby. A car was pulling into the driveway. 'Thanks for the cocoa, sweetie, but we'll pass. OK, guys, here's Daddy. We'll go home with him, and Dr Sam can use my car until morning 'cos it'd never do to have him stuck here with only two seven-year-olds and six cats as chaperons.' She kissed Susie lightly on the nose and headed for the door. 'Lots of choices, sweetie,' she said. 'You remember that.'

'Tell me again why you're doing this?' Sam asked.

Cocoa hadn't cut it in the hunger stakes. Susie had whipped him up an omelette while Sam had tucked the twins into their sleeping bags in Elsie's spare room. He'd had to boot two cats off one bed and four off the other, but he was pretty much sure that the moment he got downstairs the cats would be right back in.

'I told Elsie I would. She'll fret about her cats all the time she's away if I don't. And the boys are used to babysitting people's houses. Sometimes it's even a relief to get away from Brenda's television. Not that Brenda isn't great, but…'

'What happened to Brenda?' he asked. Brenda's IQ was that of about a nine-year-old, he thought. Functionally she was great but there was definitely mental impairment.

'She wandered into the surf when she was two,' Susie said. 'She was resuscitated—it was a major miracle that they saved her life—but she's always had problems.'

'So you'll look after her for ever?'

'Of course I will.'

'You're responsible for everyone.'

'Nope,' she said.

'No? How long have you had off the island?'

'Almost six years,' she said. 'While I trained.'

'Tell me you didn't come home every weekend during your training.'

'I came home every weekend during my training,' she agreed. 'But then I went to London.'

'Which was a disaster.'

'My twins are not a disaster.'

'No,' he said. 'But your only time away from here made you even more tied to the place.'

'I like it here.'

'You'd never move?'

'No.'

'Because you like it, or because you feel responsible?'

'A bit of both,' she admitted. 'Sam, thank you for your help tonight, but I need to go to bed. Maybe you'd better go.'

'Not before I ask you to marry me.'

Yeah, well, so much for plans. He'd intended to do this outside. He wanted a bit of romance here. A full moon with moonbeams glinting over the water. The hush-hush of surf washing in and out on a sun-warmed beach. A palm tree or two waving in the wind, maybe a violin…

Instead he was wiping dishes while Susie washed, in Elsie's fussy, ornament-laden kitchen, with two weird cats winding themselves round and round his legs.

'What?' Susie said faintly. A man had to do something here, fast. He lifted her hands from the suds and dried them with his dishcloth while she stared at him with stunned bemusement, then he set the cloth down, swung her up in his arms and kicked the back door open.

He damn near killed them both tripping over another cat as he strode outside.

Hell, this was the wrong place. There wasn't even any beach here. You couldn't see the sea through the trees from Elsie's back porch.

There was a hen house too close to the back door. As he stumbled outside, the chooks responded with startled alarm, clucking at a volume he wasn't aware chooks were capable of.

Thwarted, he set Susie down on the back step and stared out into the night in bemusement.

'Um…what's going on?' Susie said faintly.

'I'm trying to find somewhere romantic.'

'Don't,' she said, and she sounded frightened.

He gave up on the romance. Frightening her was the last thing he wanted to do.

He sat down beside her and tried to take her hand. She snatched it away as if it burned. 'Sam, no.'

'I'm making a pig's breakfast of this,' he said ruefully.

'Then stop. Now.'

'I need to ask you to marry me.'

There was a sharp intake of breath. 'Sam, no.'

'But I've fallen in love with you,' he said simply. 'I know this isn't the right time. I know it should be a candlelit dinner with violins in the background, or at the end of a moonlit cruise with me on bended knee or…or…Hell,' he said simply. 'I have no idea. All I know, Susie, is that I've fallen desperately in love with you. I can't think of anything else. I haven't been able to think of anything else for days now and it's driving me nuts. This afternoon over on the mainland I bought a ring. It's not even the right size. I don't know what sort of ring you like. But I bought it anyway.'

He lifted it from his pocket and flipped the lid open. It lay nestled on black velvet. It consisted of a simple band of gold with one solitary diamond, dead centre. It was the biggest diamond he could afford. It was a truly stunning diamond.

'This is probably wrong,' he said softly. 'The jeweller said I could use it for the occasion and you can come in later and change it for anything you like—anything in the whole shop—

anything in the country. I don't care. But I needed something tangible to show you that it's real. Susie, Grant gave you only promises, and he lied. He can't have loved you. I know he messed with you. I know he's my twin and I know my appearance must mess with your head. But I love you more than anything in the world and I just wanted to say…Look, I'll shut up. I'm making a botch of this. But I just thought…I had to ask…Please.'

She stared down at the ring. Yeah, it should be moonlight. Elsie had a porch light but she also had a mosquito zapper, a horrible blue fluorescent buzzing thing that zapped intermittently behind them. Its light made the diamond look blue. OK, it made everything look blue.

It was the most beautiful thing she'd ever seen.

It was way, way too big.

She couldn't. It was impossible. It was over-the-top ridiculous. But she'd hold this moment to her for the rest of her life, she thought. For this moment, with this man, life was perfect.

Maybe she could even say yes.

She couldn't, and she knew she couldn't, but oh, she so wanted to.

She sniffed.

'Don't you dare cry,' Sam said,

'Wh-why not?'

'Because I don't have a handkerchief,' he said desperately. 'I don't have anything. No moonlight, no surf, no violins, no bended knee—how the hell can a man kneel on bended knee when you're sitting on the second step? And, Susie, I want you more than anything in the world and I'd give you anything but right here, right now, I don't have a handkerchief. I gave it to Elsie when she was saying goodbye to her cats. So…'

'Sam?' She was half laughing, half crying, looking up at him with her eyes alight with love and laughter. 'Sam?'

'Yes?'

'Just kiss me,' she said, and so he did.

They surfaced to cats. At some subconscious level—it must have been way down, for he was kissing Susie and there wasn't a lot of room left for anything else—he could feel fur sinuously trailing around his legs. He was sitting on the step with Susie in his arms, and the cats moved from nuzzling their ankles to jumping into their laps. That was still not enough to interfere with what was really important, but then a cheeky black and white, three-quarter-grown kitten pushed its head in between their tangled arms and pushed against their chins. They broke apart laughing. Sam lifted the kitten, held it out over the balustrade until he knew it had its balance and then let it drop into the flower-bed.

Two seconds later it was back, eager to continue this game.

'No,' Sam said, and held it out again.

Susie withdrew a little, still laughing, but her eyes were growing sober.

'The cat's right,' she said.

'Sure, the cat's right,' he said. 'The cat wants to kiss you. But that's my prerogative.'

'It's not.'

'No?' he said, and suddenly the laughter was gone.

'No.'

'You're not saying no, are you?'

'I think I must.'

He nodded, cautious now. Aware that he hadn't got it right. But would there ever be a right way to approach something as complicated as this? Or as important?

'Susie, I've done my homework,' he said.

'That's...that's good.'

'This isn't an idle offer. It's for real.'

'That's what—'

'That's what Grant said,' he finished for her. 'I know. I'd give anything not to be fighting the ghost of my twin on this, but somehow I am and I need to get it right. It's one of the reasons I bought the ring before I asked you. It's the most expensive ring in the whole damned shop. I had to make you see…'

'It is pretty big.'

'Susie, I need to finish saying this.'

'There's no point.' She sounded breathless and desperate. She was backing away now for real, pushing herself along the step so she was hard against the balustrade. He made no move to draw her back. This was the time for words, he thought.

He had to get this right.

'I've been in Melbourne,' he said inconsequentially, and maybe it was the right thing to say because she stared at him, puzzled. The desperation became confusion.

'In Melbourne.'

'I've been sweating on this,' he told her. 'Trying to see how we could work this. This island's not big enough to support us all. I can't work full time as a doctor here, and I have a feeling our family's only going to get more expensive.'

'What the—'

'Let me finish,' he said. 'Just hear me out. Susie, I was trying to figure out how I could work here. I know you won't leave the island, and your commitment here, to Brenda, to the boys, is part of who you are. I love you just as you are, so trying to change such a huge part of you is never going to happen.'

'Then…'

'Just listen,' he told her, and he put a finger on her lips to enforce her silence. 'The first thing I did was go and see the local council,' he said. 'Nick came with me. We figured there needed to be some representation about how urgent it is to get the bridge fixed, and maybe upgraded. What we found was that the council is half-hearted about even repairing the single-lane bridge.'

'I knew this would happen. I knew it.' She stood up and stared down at him, distressed. 'As soon as I saw the damage…'

'This is my story,' he said. 'Let me finish.' She looked lovely, he thought. Just beautiful. And the knowledge that what he was about to say would take away her distress was wonderful. 'Anyway while we were there the local mayor received a phone call,' he said, while she stared down at him, bewildered. 'He got pretty excited and came to find the roads engineer while we were in his office. You remember Carly and Pete Hammond?'

'Of course I do. The guy in the boat.'

'His boat was worth a fortune,' Sam said. 'He'd just picked it up from the dealer. It wasn't even insured yet, but that hasn't bothered them. Carly Hammond is the heiress of some biscuit empire, Pete's a financier and they're loaded.'

'But…'

'Hush,' he told her, feeling the need to sound severe. 'Anyway, it seems Pete's going to be OK. The doctors in Melbourne have been praising you to the skies—your fast work saved his life and made his injuries a sight less serious than they could have been. Anyway, in post-trauma gratitude to everyone who helped, Carly rang the mayor and asked if there was anything the island needed. The mayor, half joking, said a double-laned bridge would be nice. She said, "Done." The mayor couldn't believe it. Anyway, he was coming to get a rough guesstimate of the cost of the bridge from the engineer. Nick and I were standing there with our mouths open. The engineer named a sum that seemed astronomical, the mayor rang Carly back and she said the cheque's in the mail.'

There was a moment's stupefied silence. 'I don't believe it,' Susie said at last, but Sam knew that she did.

'I had to practically blackmail Nick into not telling you,'

Sam told her, grinning. 'The mayor wasn't saying anything until the cheque arrived—he thought Carly was probably nuts—but it arrived this afternoon, and the bank's already cleared it.'

'Oh,' Susie said faintly, and sat down again.

'And it all fits,' Sam said. 'Because I'd already talked to the authorities at the hospital in Sandridge. It seems this area is in crying need of a new orthopaedic surgeon. The guy there has been threatening retirement for a decade.'

'You wouldn't,' she breathed.

'I couldn't be an orthopaedic surgeon over there when there's no bridge,' he agreed. 'I've been sweating over it, talking with Nick about the possibilities of owning a boat so I could get over and back, but Nick says at certain times of the year you can only get over at high tide. That's not going to work. So then I tried to figure out if I could do online teaching— anything—so I could earn a living and stay here.'

'But why?'

'Because I love you,' he said softly. 'Is that such a dumb reason? I met you less than two weeks ago and for almost two weeks I've been trying to figure out how we can work this. And it's as if the gods have planned it. The island's going to be open, Susie. Islanders will be able to get to hospital whenever they want, and visit and come home and go to Melbourne whenever they want.'

'They won't need me,' she said faintly.

'You have to be kidding,' he said strongly, and he took her hands in his and tugged her close. He half expected resistance but it didn't come. 'They love you to bits. What's the bet your pilates clinic trebles in size? You can still do the district nursing if you want but there are options all over the place. But...' He hesitated, knowing this was the most important bit, the lynchpin on which everything hung. 'But I hope I can get a look-in there. Into your future.'

'You don't want—'

'I want you, Susie,' he said strongly, his voice warm and sure. 'I love you more than anything in my life. I've been walking in fog the last couple of years, and that fog's been caused by the idea of the massive waste of Grant's illness and death. But more than that. By the waste of Grant's life. He hurt you, but in doing so he missed out on you. He missed out on the boys. His sons. Robbie and Joel. He even missed out on Brenda's curlers. Dammit, will you get away?'

The black kitten went flying again. It gave an incensed squawk as it landed in Elsie's petunias, then stalked off with its tail in the air.

Sam didn't notice. He only had eyes for Susie.

'I know you've been asked this question before,' he said. 'But not like this.'

'Not with cats,' Susie said, and miraculously the smile was back.

'Not without one single romantic plot,' he growled. 'So you have to know I'm serious.'

'You really want me?'

'The question is,' he said, letting her hands lie gently in his, holding back, trying desperately not to rush, 'do you want me?'

'Of course I want you.'

His breath came out in a whoosh. He looked into her eyes and what he saw there made his heart swell within his chest. His Susie. His one true love.

'Effie's coming tomorrow,' he told her. 'My crazy, lovely great-aunt. She's coming to check you out, and to check out the twins. I've already told her you're a darling. Can I tell her you'll also be my wife?'

'Would you really want to tell her that?'

'More than anything in the world.'

'Then you'd better tell her,' she said, smiling and smiling. 'Oh, Sam, you're my happy ending.'

'Don't you believe it,' he growled. She was too beautiful to resist kissing for a moment longer. He tugged her into his arms and he kissed her as he'd ached to kiss her for too long. He held her close, he loved her and when the kitten finally found the courage to shove in again its cause was lost.

There wasn't an inch of room for a kitten to shove its nose anywhere.

CHAPTER TWELVE

HE KISSED her and he went home.

She wanted him to stay. Elsie's bedroom was strange and lonely. She and Sam were two mature adults who'd decided this night to marry. If he'd lifted her up and carried her to bed she'd have reacted with nothing but joy.

'But it's not going to happen,' he rumbled into her hair as she tentatively suggested it. 'We didn't think this through and we're not prepared. I'm damned if tomorrow morning you will think for one moment you might be left in the mess Grant left you in. I'll not spoil this. I'll sleep at Doris's again, and we'll discuss important stuff in the morning.'

It was the one discordant note. That he should think of Grant then…For she'd forgotten.

For the first couple of days after she'd met Sam, her image of Grant had been crazily intertwined with this person she knew as Sam. But Grant was gone. His ghost wasn't hanging around to trouble her. Sam was her new love, her future. Sure, he was Grant's twin but Grant was her past and to mix them any more…It didn't make sense.

But she wasn't arguing. She let him go, kissing him fiercely, possessively as he drew away, and she watched until his car lights disappeared into the distance and then she tried to sleep.

She was wearing Sam's ring.

It was too big. It was too loose on her finger. It was too…expensive.

He'd only bought her that because of Grant, too, she thought, and there was another discordant note.

But he loved her. That was the huge thing. He'd fallen in love with her and she loved him with an intensity she'd never believed she was capable of. That he loved her kids…that he loved this island and wanted to stay and be part of it…that the new bridge would be built and the islanders could be part of the real world without leaving their beloved homes…It was too much to take in. She lay and stared out of Elsie's window and wished she was home so she could go and tell Brenda or sit on her swing and tell the sea…

A soft thump on the end of the bed announced the arrival of a cat. It purred its way along her body until it reached her pillow. It was the kitten that had given Sam trouble tonight.

'I'm getting married, cat,' she told it. 'Sam loves me and he's given me this ring and we're going to live happily ever after.'

The cat stared at her in the moonlight, its eyes thoughtful.

'Don't you dare tell me not to let my heart sway my head,' she said. 'I know cats work on the cupboard principle but we work on a higher plane.'

Oh, yeah? The kitten started kneading the coverlet, where a million pulled threads told Susie that this was a nightly event.

'I'm not being dumb,' Susie told the cat, and then wondered where that thought had come from. Why was she worried?

She put her hand out from the covers and held it out so she could see her ring. It really was…extravagant.

'He's just covering all bases,' she told the cat. 'He's wonderful.'

The cat gazed at her for another long moment. It was Susie who broke their stare.

'I'm being dumb, worrying,' she told the cat, but the cat, having won the stare-off, was already asleep.

She'd said yes.

Sam didn't go straight home. He took himself down to the beach and walked and walked, until he was too weary to walk any longer. She'd said yes.

He wanted to be with her, right now. She'd offered. She'd wanted to.

But he had to get this right. She was coming from Grant to him. He had to show her that he was different.

How could Grant have ever treated her like that? The thought of Susie, bereft and pregnant, alone in London, made him feel sick.

But he had the power to make it right. And she loved him.

She loved him.

The thought brought a wash of joy so fierce it almost blew him away. She loved him. She'd marry him.

Tomorrow Effie would come and he'd introduce Susie as his fiancée. It would bring joy to the old lady, he thought, as his news tonight would bring pleasure to most of the islanders.

And he could make this work. He could bring the medical situation on this island up to the best available anywhere in the world. Sandridge hospital was a good one. There were some decent doctors there, and Joe tonight had said that once the bridge was built and this island became accessible for living on, the place would grow. He and Susie could expand her pilates clinic. They could bring a family doctor over here a few times a week—maybe one might even live here.

Maybe Effie would stay.

And he and Susie and the twins could have their happy ever after.

Despite Grant.

Grant was still there. He still worried him. He had to banish his ghost from this happy ever after and keep him banished.

'It's over,' he told his twin's ghost, and he turned back to the car. Dammit, he should have stayed with Susie tonight. He'd wanted to so badly.

'I'm not like Grant,' he said, and turned and tossed a great lump of driftwood as far as he could out into the waves. 'I'm not, and I'll be letting Susie see that for the rest of our lives.'

He didn't ring.

Yeah, well, that'd be because Effie was coming this morning and he had to catch the boat over at high tide to go and meet her. But at nine as the first of her islanders filed into the pilates room Susie was aware of a stab of disappointment.

She should have rung him. But…he was calling the tune!

Doris came in limping, muttering about stupid boarders who'd left stupid boots where an old lady might trip over them, and Susie didn't even scold her about the amount of miscellaneous clutter she stored in her living room. She let her settle into easy arm exercises, stretching the muscles and stabilising the neck. She wasn't chatty. Muriel and Lionel were working on the other machines. They were hardly chatty either.

'Susie, what are you wearing on your finger?' Muriel asked, and her voice was a faint squeak. 'Is that what I think it is?'

'It's a diamond,' Susie said defensively. She'd been in two minds whether to wear it this morning—she was starting to feel like there were things she needed to sort out with Sam before she made things public. But the thought of leaving it at Elsie's place seemed wrong. Did she drive home before her clinic and leave it there? Did she not wear it?

In the end it had seemed easiest to slip it onto her finger and deal with the consequences later. Did she want to marry Sam?

Yes, she did. And he'd asked her, hadn't he, so where was the problem? It was only this dumb little niggle that surfaced every time she looked at his oversized diamond.

The dumb little niggle was pushed firmly into the file in her head marked 'Later'.

'Sam's asked you to marry him?' Doris breathed.

'Yes,' she said, almost defiant.

'And the bridge is being fixed,' Lionel whispered, breathless with excitement.

'You're not supposed to know that,' Muriel snapped.

'Neither are you,' Lionel retorted. 'But the whole island knew by breakfast-time.'

'There aren't any secrets on this island,' Doris said, hauling her arms out of her straps and fixing her gaze on Susie. 'Or there aren't supposed to be. When did this happen?'

'You tell me,' Susie said, and tried to smile, but it didn't come off.

'It must have been last night. But he slept in his own bed last night.'

'Hey,' she said, flushing. Too much information.

'He asked you to marry him last night?' Muriel demanded.

'I… Yes.'

'Good girl,' Lionel said, and beamed, but Doris and Muriel had already moved on.

'You sent him home to bed after he asked you to marry him. Are you out of your mind?' Doris demanded.

'I'm a good girl,' she tried, but the women weren't biting.

'You're a woman. And he's a man in a million and things weren't what they were when we were young. Not that I'd have sent my Harold home,' Doris said. 'So why did you?'

'It's none of your—'

'It'll be because of the twins,' Muriel said doubtfully. 'She won't want to shock them.'

'He was parked in front of my place at midnight,' Doris retorted. 'He went down to the beach and walked for hours. I woke up for my three a.m. cup of tea and he was out there, walking. The twins would have been solidly asleep at three a.m.'

'Why weren't you with him?' Muriel demanded.

'Hey,' Susie said, starting to get angry. 'I just told you that I'm getting married. Aren't you happy for me?'

'Of course we're happy for you,' Doris retorted. 'But why did you send him home?'

'I didn't send him home.'

'You didn't?'

'No.'

There was a baffled silence. No one could think of anything to say.

'Back to work,' Susie tried, but it didn't come out right.

'His aunt's coming today,' Muriel said, ignoring her. 'I'll talk to her.'

'You'll do no such thing.'

'I'll have Harold talk to Sam, then,' she said. 'You don't even have your grandpa to protect you.'

'What could he possibly have to protect me from? Sam's wonderful.'

'He is,' Muriel said.

'He's got shadows,' Doris said.

'Shadows or not, he shoulda stayed,' Lionel said. 'Things aren't what they used to be in my day if a fella like Sam excuses himself and goes home to bed after buying a girl a ring. Not without a damned good argument to the contrary.' He sighed. 'Well, well. Times have changed. Adjust these straps, will you, Susie, love? If the younger generation's falling apart, we'll just have to hang round a bit longer to put you right.'

* * *

Susie didn't see Sam till that night. At about four he phoned and asked if he could bring Effie to dinner. 'Barbecue on the beach?' he asked, and she thought he sounded a bit strained.

'I need to talk to you,' she said.

'You're still wearing my ring?'

'Of course.'

'I love you,' he said, and the world settled again. Her anxieties stilled. It'd be fine.

'I can come now,' he said, but she'd promised to pop in and see Donna's baby tonight. Chloe had a rash.

He loved her. Talking could wait. Rashes and anxious mothers couldn't.

'Bring your aunt to our place at six,' she said, smiling. 'We'll be ready. I'll even endeavour to get the twins presentable.'

'There's no need,' he said. 'Effie will love you all as you are.'

Before she could respond he'd disconnected. She replaced the phone in her pocket, feeling better. Almost OK. Just not…not…

She didn't know what. Maybe it was Grant, she thought. Maybe promises to marry could never be the same again.

But it was nothing to do with Grant. She knew that. This was all about Sam. Sam and her. Happy ever after.

What was wrong? What?

She shoved her disquiet into the background and went on working.

By the time she got home she was in a rush. A simple barbecue…Yeah, but she wanted the steak to be good and be marinaded and she wanted to do special salads and a yummy dessert and she just felt…breathless.

By the time she opened the door to Effie and Sam she was really puffed. And then she was…astounded.

Effie was round and dumpy and beaming. Her wispy white hair was secured into a knot on the top of her head, but the knot wasn't very secure. She wore John Lennon glasses which looked more at home on Effie than they ever had on John Lennon. But John Lennon had never let society dictate his dress, and obviously neither had Effie. The hair and the glasses were her sole concession to her age. For the rest...

She wore what looked like vast silky harem pants in shimmering lavender, a pink blouse and a violet shawl with pink dragons embroidered on with silk.

Her fingernails were long and pink, with tiny white dragons painted on every finger.

She was wearing pink and white slippers with toes that curled up and over, like someone from Aladdin's Cave.

Susie blinked.

'Hi,' Sam said from behind his aunt. He set Effie gently aside, reached forward, took Susie into his arms and kissed her. Then he drew her round to face Effie. 'This is Susie,' he said.

'You know, I'd guessed that,' Effie said warmly, and she stood on tiptoe to give Susie a kiss of her own. 'Sam's told me so much.'

'All of it good, I hope,' she said, knowing she sounded nervous, not able to do anything about it.

'Oh, my goodness,' Effie said, looking behind her. For there were Joel and Robbie, coming shyly out from the living room, ready to greet Sam with joy but brought up short by the appearance of this lady they didn't know.

'It's the twins,' Effie said, and burst into tears.

It was a very happy, very silly evening. For a lady who should be suffering from jet-lag, Effie was amazing. She set herself to enjoy her first barbecue on an Australian beach with such gusto that the success of the night was assured.

Sam seemed quiet, but he didn't have much choice, Susie thought as the evening wore on. Effie and the twins held sway, with Brenda chipping in more than she usually did as Effie's enthusiasm disarmed them all.

They ate steak and salad and lamingtons and pavlova and piles and piles of grapes. Susie had provided beer and wine but Effie's only concession to her jet-lag was that she avoid alcohol, so they all had lemonade.

After dinner the twins and Sam swam, while Effie paddled and splashed in the shallows. They played beach cricket and the boys found, to their astonishment, that their first kindly ball bowled to this gentle old lady led to a long-distance swim to retrieve it.

They played until dusk turned almost to darkness. Brenda retired to her television, and Sam carried two sleepy little boys to bed.

'Let me do it,' he told Susie, kissing her gently before picking up a twin in each arm to bear them bodily inside. 'I need to get good at this.'

Susie watched them go, this man she loved and her kids that she adored. It would work. It must.

'It's a miracle,' Effie whispered beside her, and Susie returned her attention to her guest. She'd spread a rug and cushions on the sand in deference to Effie's long journey and advanced age, but until now Effie had scorned to use them. But with Sam inside, she relaxed, sinking down onto the cushions, stretching like a cat and gazing up at the emerging stars in wonder. 'I never saw this happening.'

'He was engaged before, wasn't he?' Susie said tentatively, not sure what the rules here were, but Effie answered without hesitation.

'To Marilyn. I knew they weren't right. Sagittarius. What are you, dear?'

'Virgo.'

'Perfect. Just perfect.'

'It's not just star signs,' Susie ventured, and got a sharp nod in response.

'I'd be the first to agree. But it does count. I'm not saying you can't make it work when the stars are against you but it makes it so much harder. And you can fight your star sign, too. Like Grant. He came out like he resented where he'd been born. Did you know Sam was three minutes older? I'm thinking Grant begrudged him those three minutes all his life.'

'It can't have made much difference.'

'Of course it could,' Effie said. 'Sam was the older one. He was responsible. Those parents of his…they spelt it out. Grant was charming and…I don't know. Effervescent. Like some sort of glittering illusion. Even when he was little he used to manipulate people's emotions and Sam would be left to deal with the mess. Mind, he had to deal with the mess his mother left as well, which was even harder. His mother walked out when the twins were five, and you would have thought it was all Sam's fault. My brother was a hard man. I don't say he deserved what he got, but he was austere and relentless in what he saw as his duty. He knew he didn't stand a chance with Grant—Grant simply ignored him, giggled, did what he wanted. I had a theory for a while that the child was slightly autistic—he didn't feel like we did. He stayed mostly with his mother but when he was too much for her he came back to us. My brother could chastise all he wanted, shout, even weep, but Grant went on regardless. It was up to Sam to try and fix things.'

'Why are you telling me this?' Susie asked. She glanced across at the twins' lighted window. Sam was in there, reading the twins their bedtime story. It seemed wrong that she be out here, gossiping about his past.

'Because he's finally fixed it,' Effie said, and stretched again, sinking deeper into her pile of pillows. 'And this is the end.'

Susie frowned. She stopped looking at Sam's profile inside the house and turned to look at Effie. Effie was contentedly stargazing, relaxed and at ease.

'The end of what?' she asked cautiously.

'Grant's messes,' Effie said. Jet-lag must be finally catching up with her. Her voice was getting a bit dreamy, as if drifting toward sleep. 'You have no idea…There was cheating, bullying, stealing, love affairs with girls who were distraught, university records where results were fabricated…What Grant wanted, he got, and everywhere he went he left a mess Sam had to clean up. My brother gave up in the end and never lifted a finger to stop the worst of Grant's excesses. But the consequences would tear him apart. So Sam would step in. Shield his father from the knowledge of the worst of it. Even I wasn't allowed to see the worst.'

'Is that right?' Susie said, in a voice that wasn't quite steady.

'My brother died just before Grant was diagnosed with leukaemia,' Effie said. 'Well, it was dreadful, but there wasn't anything we could do about it. Not even Sam, try as he might. Leukaemia was one mess that wasn't of Grant's making. One mess that no one could sort out. Then Grant died and I thought I might lose Sam, too. Sam's been the responsible one, over and over, and when Grant died…he was devastated. It was like one last mess that Sam couldn't fix. He couldn't sort it, you see. There was nothing left he could do to make it right.'

'I…I see.'

'And now there's you.' Effie's voice was deeply slurred now, sleep finally catching up with her. 'Grant's left you and he's left your beautiful little boys. Grant's sons. So this is one last thing Sam can do. He can take this last mess made by Grant and he can make it right. He can put Grant to rest with this last piece of ghastly chaos that Grant's created. He can take you under his wing, he can take on this last piece of responsibility and find his happy ending in the process. Oh, Susie, my beloved Sam is happy, and now, if you'll excuse me, I think I might be falling asleep.'

* * *

Something was wrong.

The night had been fantastic, Sam thought, but as soon as he emerged from the house he knew things had changed.

Effie was almost asleep, and Susie was looking at him with eyes that were clouded. She was schooling her expression into one as neutral as possible, but he was close enough to her now to sense there was trouble.

'What's wrong?' he asked without preamble.

'What could be wrong?' she said, but he could hear the effort she was making to keep her voice light. 'Effie's so tired she's almost unconscious. You need to take her home to bed.'

'I'll take her home and come back.'

'No,' she said. 'I have a headache.'

'You get headaches?'

'Yes.'

'Bad headaches?'

'I have a bad headache now.'

'I have aspirin in my purse,' Effie offered sleepily. 'And a little round crystal you rub on your temple. And a vial of lavender oil.'

'I just need to go to sleep,' Susie said. 'I was in the wrong bed last night and didn't get enough sleep.'

'Whose bed did you sleep in?' Effie asked, waking up.

'Not Sam's,' she said bluntly. 'Because Sam doesn't want to be like Grant.'

Sam frowned. What the hell…? 'Susie…'

'Take Effie home,' she said wearily.

'I'll come back later.'

'No.' She picked up a couple of cushions and held them like a shield.

'Is there anything I can—?'

'No. I need to go to bed. Please,' she said shortly, and headed up to the veranda. She was aware that she sounded rude but there wasn't anything she could do about it.

'Susie, what's wrong?' he demanded again, starting to feel really concerned.

'You're the doctor,' she snapped. She winced and pressed fingers on her temple and tried a smile. 'Sorry. We have an exercise physiologist, a doctor and an astrologer here, so I guess we're equipped for any diagnosis but the long and short of it is that I have a headache caused by lack of sleep. And if Effie doesn't go to bed soon I imagine she'll have a headache worse than mine. So I'll bid you goodnight.'

'Goodnight, dear,' Effie said, pausing doubtfully as Sam helped her to her feet. 'I hope I haven't said anything…wrong.'

'What did you say?' Sam demanded, sounding ominous.

'Nothing,' Susie interjected fast. 'How could Effie have said anything wrong? But I'm sorry. I don't want to be rude but I really do need to go to bed.' Sam stepped forward, clearly intending to kiss her goodnight, but she stepped away fast and held her cushions closer.

'No.'

'Susie—'

'Just go,' she said, and walked inside and closed the door behind her.

'What the hell did you say to her?' Sam demanded as the porch light flicked off. They were being told to leave in no uncertain terms.

'I just talked about how happy I was,' Effie said, bewildered.

'Nothing else?'

'I don't think so. I was almost asleep. I just said how nice it was that you were happy.'

'Effie—'

'Sam, I'm old,' Effie said, reverting to an excuse she'd used before in sticky situations where she wasn't quite sure of her ground. 'If Susan's tired, I dare say I'm more so. Maybe I'll remember in the morning. For now…can you take me back to Doris's or I'll fall asleep where I'm standing.'

Susie's door was closed. Her bedroom light flickered on, but the blind was tugged closed before he saw her, and darkness prevailed.

'I need to talk to her,' Sam said.

'In the morning,' Effie told him. 'I need my bed.'

She had notes to write. A lot of notes. Stuff to pack. Things to do.

Half an hour after Sam had left her cellphone rang. She checked that it wasn't someone in trouble—no matter how urgent her affairs were tonight, if there was a medical emergency and she didn't respond, she'd never forgive herself. But the incoming number was Sam's.

She flicked the cell through to the message bank, took herself into the storeroom where there were no windows to reveal to an outside world that someone might be awake, and went on writing.

What the hell was going on? Sam made Effie comfortable, rang Susie, rang her again, and then drove back. Her house was in darkness.

Maybe she did have a headache. Maybe she'd gone to sleep.

Headache. Subarachnoid haemorrhage. Stroke.

Frustrated and worried, he banged on the front door. A curlered head poked out the nearest window.

'What do you want?'

'I'm worried about Susie,' he told Brenda, and Brenda glowered.

'We're all in bed. We're OK.'

'Is Susie OK?'

'Of course she's OK.'

'Will you check?'

The curlers disappeared. From the innards of the house, Brenda's voice boomed, loud enough to wake the dead.

'Susie, are you OK?'

'I'm trying to sleep.' Susie's voice answered in the distance, and Brenda's head appeared again.

'She's trying to sleep. Go away.'

The head disappeared, the window slammed shut and the house reverted to darkness.

She couldn't face him, she thought desperately as she wrote. If she went outside he'd hold her and make it all right. He'd make her fears seem groundless.

She was no one's mess.

She kept on writing.

Nick always left just before dawn when he was heading to sea for a couple of nights. The fisherman drove across the island in darkness, pulling up at the wharf. His assistant was waiting, John—a likely lad of a little over seventy. And so was Susie, sitting on a suitcase, huddled into an overcoat, as pale as death.

'She says she's coming with us,' John said unhappily. 'She says she's walking out on the twins.'

'I'm walking out on everyone,' Susie said, standing up and heaving her suitcase across onto the deck of Nick's boat. 'I need a lift to the mainland.'

'Why the hell—?' Nick said.

'I've left you all notes,' Susie said. 'I'll be back in two weeks but, Nick, if you dare phone and tell anyone, and I mean anyone, including Donna, what I'm doing until I'm well away from here then I won't come back in two weeks. So help me, Nick, I mean it.'

'You have to come back,' John said unhappily.

'I will,' she promised. 'Of course I will. Because I'm responsible. But for the next two weeks I intend to be very irresponsible indeed.'

The twins woke up to notes—one on each of their pillows.

Hi, guys. I'm off on an adventure. I was thinking last night about all the adventures you two have. How you go off with Nick and Bobbie and Lisa and camp on the other side of the island. How you go to Scout camp. How you have sleepovers at your friends' places. And suddenly I thought, I haven't had an adventure for a very long time. Mummies work really hard. We clean and we cook and we look after people, and sometimes we get tired. I'm like that now. I'm really, really tired, so I've decided to have an adventure. I'm going to stay in a big hotel in Sydney for fourteen sleeps and do adventuring things. I'll phone you every night and I'll send you postcards, and when I come back I'll be ready to go back to being a mummy.

Donna and Brenda will look after you and make sure you have fun while I'm away. Sam and his nice Aunty Effie will help look after you, too.

There are lots of lamingtons in the fridge and you can help Brenda shop for the things you like to eat. I love you a lot. Be good and have adventures of your own while I'm away.

Mum.

Donna and Brenda woke up to notes, too. They were still taking them in when Sam found and read his. Sam's had been stuck under Doris's front door, and Doris only found it after she'd called him for breakfast. She handed it to Sam, then stood by wordlessly as he read.

Dear Sam

Last night was a revelation. I knew this was too good to be true. I thought I fell in love with Grant, but I was wrong. I didn't know what love was. And then I thought I fell in love with you. Maybe I did, but I was just as dumb as I was eight years ago.

Because I don't want what you're offering.

Or maybe I do. But just for a bit. Maybe I can use what you're offering in the only way I can accept. I'll take your help to alleviate your conscience, whatever your stupid conscience is saying.

Here it is. You can take it on, all my responsibilities, the twins, Brenda, the medical needs of the island, the pilates clinic. This is what Effie says you want, a chance to make Grant's mess right, but you don't have to marry me to do it. I don't want anything to do with any relationship with this hanging over it.

Sam, I met Grant a long time ago. I had my twins because of him and, yes, I'll accept his money so the boys' future is secure. I'll even use a little bit for what I'm planning over the next two weeks. But I'm not Grant's mess, and neither are my boys. As for marrying you to clear up after Grant... No.

So I'm leaving. I've thought it through and I'm not negotiating. I'm just telling you.

For two weeks I'm having no responsibilities. Not one. I'm leaving all of you to take care of each other. I've written to the boys explaining what's happening and they'll be OK with it—they go on school camps and they know the drill. Even though their mother has never left them before, they're old enough to know the concept of two weeks and they'll survive. I've written to Donna and to Brenda and they'll know what to do, too. They both owe me heaps and this is my two weeks for calling in debts.

And now it's all yours. Medicine for one island, for two weeks, to alleviate Grant's last mess. Meanwhile, I'm out of here. I'm going to sleep on the beach, have massages, read books. I'm going to take care of me. This can be your debt to clear your head of Grant. You can take over all my responsibilities and give me space to have a break I haven't had since I got pregnant.

And that's it. Enough. I'm damned if I'll let you use me to sort out your head. In two weeks I'll be back, but I'll get to the mainland wharf and I'll ring and I'll check that you're off the island. If you're still here then I'm waiting until you leave before I return. In two weeks' time you walk away and you don't look back. Your responsibility is over. I don't care that it does your head in, Sam. It's my life and you don't come near me.

All the best, to you and to Effie. Of course you'll be welcome to keep in touch with the twins whenever you want. If you want to take the job on the mainland then you're welcome to do that, too. I can't stop you. But you're not welcome in my life.

Thank you for the ring, but it was ostentatious and it was stupid. I'll deposit it in a bank in Sydney and send you the details of where you can collect it.

All the best.

Susan.

He stared at the note blindly for a long minute. Then he swore, handed the letter to a confounded Doris, and went and hauled open Effie's bedroom door.

'Effie,' he said, very softly indeed. 'Tell me exactly what you told Susie.'

CHAPTER THIRTEEN

A LIFE of luxury and indolent ease wasn't as great as it was cut out to be. Not when your heart was broken. Not when you felt sick about what you'd left behind. Not when you haven't ever had anything to do with indolence and ease and didn't know what the heck to do with it.

Susie caught the early train to Melbourne. She then caught a plane to Northern Queensland. She'd told the boys she was going to Sydney, but by the time she was halfway to the mainland she'd figured Sydney was too close and the islanders would likely arrive in force and haul her home.

Or—more likely—Sam would come and start making his stupid protestations again.

When she got to Cairns she went into the tourist information centre and got directions to the most luxurious resort on the coast. Grant's money was burning a hole in her bank account and he at least owed her. Two weeks of luxury wouldn't deprive her boys of an education. Dammit, she deserved it.

At the resort she told them she was travelling incognito and to deny her presence there to anyone.

'No matter what,' she said. 'My family have my cellphone number. They can text me in an emergency but I want contact with no one else.'

At seven each night she rang the twins. If anyone else answered she was polite—'Brenda, this is my holiday and this call is expensive. Can you put the boys on please.' 'Donna, I'm fine, but I need space. Can you put the boys on, please.'

Once Sam answered and she hung up.

He texted. They all did—the whole damned island. She did a cursory first-line check twice a day that there wasn't an emergency and then deleted them all.

The time was hers.

She slept late the first day—that was to be expected as she hadn't slept the night before. She woke at eleven and was pleased. This was what a holiday was meant to be. Lots of luxurious sleep.

She wandered down to the beach and swam. She ate lunch, trying to stretch it out to be leisurely, but it was pretty hard to have a leisurely lunch with no one to talk to.

She chose a book from the resort library and lay under a palm tree and read.

She went for a long walk on the beach.

She wondered if the kids had gone to Sea Scouts.

She tried not to check her phone.

She wondered who'd taken her pilates clinic. No one. It'd be cancelled. If Doris didn't keep those legs moving…

Stopitstopitstopit.

She ate dinner under the palms at a candlelit table, the warm wind whispering through the palm fronds. She watched honeymooning couples.

She tried not to check her phone.

She went to bed early, slept restlessly, woke at five a.m and thought about Sam.

OK, so a life of indolence and ease wasn't going to cut it. There was an activity board at Reception. Snorkelling. Surf kites. Horseriding.

How many activities could she fit into one day?
How early did the first activity start?

'Her calls are being tracked from far north Queensland. How many hotels are in your area? That many? OK, let's start with the most expensive and work down.'

Nocturnal walks, nature spotting included. Total head count—one startled possum caught in floodlights. She could have seen a hundred of them at home.

Movies. What about something gory? No? How many honeymoon couples did they have staying in this place?

'She won't be using her real name. You'll know her. She's gorgeous and she's desperately lonely and I love her to bits. I've hurt her. I just need to know…No. Of course not. Only couples? Yes, I see. Thank you anyway.'

'So massage is the only thing I haven't tried? I don't think I want…Well, if you're sure. Yeah, I know it can be remedial. I guess I am stressed. And it's only for medical purposes. I'm a nurse, you know. I can stay with my clothes…No, I guess I can't. Well, if you're sure…'

'Dr Sam Renaldo. Yes, from the US, but this is a family matter. We're looking for a woman called Susie, a woman who's looking bereft. The family is desperately worried about her. No, not suicidal. Not that, but…well, as a doctor I can never exclude options, and if you were personally worried about a particular guest…'

'No. No, I understand that you can't give guest details. But if your clientele is usually honeymoon couples, and there was someone on her own you felt worried about…'

'Absolutely. I understand you're telling me nothing. Absolutely. But would you have a vacant suite…?'

'I thought the massage was to be done by a woman. No, of course I'm not worried. I'm not worried. I'm not stressed. It's just…OK, let's do it. Just do it. OK, fine, I'm relaxed, dammit, just get on with it.'

Massages were supposed to be wonderful. She knew that. Properly done they could help mentally as well as physically. She was trained in exercise rehabilitation. She knew.

But it felt wrong. She lay rigid on the massage table while the masseur did his best with the knots of tension he couldn't help but be aware of.

'This is supposed to make you feel good,' he said gently as her hour-long massage moved to the ten-minute mark and the tension in her body grew and grew. It felt wrong that this man's hands were touching her. It just felt…wrong.

'I'm sorry.'

'You know, the entire staff here is worrying about you,' he told her. 'The receptionist just told me to take good care of you because you seem alone and stressed.'

'I'm not,' she said, stunned. Heck, she'd thought she was a nice anonymous guest. The occupant of Suite 9. Nothing more.

She didn't want anyone worrying about her.

'Is there anything you'd like to talk about?' her masseur queried, and she shook her head, her sense of unease growing with her sense of loneliness. She was naked apart from her skimpy panties. The man's hands were massaging the small of her back. She could feel his skill as he kneaded the rigid muscles, urging her to relax, with his words as well as his hands.

'N-no,' she muttered.

'Jodie tells me you're an exercise therapist,' he said. Jodie was the sailboard instructor. Jodie had tried to get her to talk yesterday.

'I… Yes.'

'Then you'll know that we can help—in all sorts of ways,' he said smoothly. 'Bottling troubles up can lead to major psychiatric problems.'

Great. A masseur diagnosing clinical depression. 'I'm fine,' she muttered.

'Your muscles say you're not fine.'

'Please…'

'Can I ask you to turn over?'

'No,' she snapped, feeling panicked.

'Susan, it's OK,' he said, in his best bedside manner—a manner which was starting to close in on her. 'I'm giving you a therapeutic massage. You'll stay covered at the breasts and the thighs. But you're holding yourself rigid. If you'll let me massage your abdomen I'm sure I can get you to release—'

'I don't want you to release…'

'What don't you want me to release?'

'I don't know,' she muttered. 'I just know that I don't. I should never—'

'I've pushed you too hard,' the masseur said, finally seeing her panic for the brick wall it was. 'I'm sorry. Stay on your stomach until you're comfortable.'

'I think we should stop.'

There was a pause. 'I'm expensive,' he said reluctantly. 'You've paid for an hour.'

'Look, I don't want…'

'If I finish up now, I'm in trouble,' he confessed. 'I'm new here and having a client finish a quarter of the way through reflects badly—'

'Look, I don't care.' But she did, though. Of course she did. She was responsible.

'What if I take a break for a couple of minutes? We'll both take a breather and then start again,' he said.

'Fine,' she said, resigned.

'Take three deep breaths and listen to the music,' he told her. 'It's supposed to represent the power of the sea. Think dolphins. Think power of the surf at dawn. Think peace and serenity. I'll just pop out…'

'Out you pop,' she said wearily. 'I'll still be here when you get back. I'm good like that.'

The power of the sea. Dolphins. Peace and serenity. It sounded like a cheap harp, badly played.

Relax. Get those muscles relaxed. She was wasting money if she kept being so damned tense.

She concentrated fiercely on relaxing. Relax, relax, relax.

The door opened and she tensed even more.

This guy's a paid health professional, she told herself. Relax, relax.

She heard the slight sounds of him pouring oil into his palms, warming them. He's probably been out having a fag, she thought nastily, and then felt ashamed of herself. As his hands came down on her back, she felt herself flinch.

Relax. Relax, relax.

The cigarette seemed to have done him good. He seemed surer now, smoothing the oil in long, strong strokes down the length of her spine. Sweeping strokes, over and over again, and then gentle circles on either side of her vertebrae.

This was better. This was OK.

'But I'm still not rolling over,' she muttered, and there was a moment's stillness.

'Very good call,' a beloved voice said unsteadily. 'The best call you ever made in your life. Not when you thought you were turning over for him. But would you consider turning over for me?'

Sam.

Her whole world stilled. She lay without breathing, wondering if her world would start again, wondering if she dared take a breath, and if she did so whether the wild, crazy hope would dissipate in the way of dreams.

Sam.

'Are you awake?' he asked, and went back to kneading. 'Sorry. I know the first rule of a good massage is not to get personal. Go back to what you were doing.'

She did. She could scarcely do anything else.

'Um,' she said.

'Don't talk unless you want to,' he said encouragingly. 'You're the client. My aim is to serve you in every way possible.'

'What have you done with my masseur?' she tried, and was ridiculously pleased that her voice didn't squeak.

'I sent him home for the day,' he said. 'A hundred Australian dollars. He gave up massaging you for a hundred dollars. The man's out of his mind.'

'How did you find me?' His hands were doing amazing things to her spine. She wasn't moving. She couldn't move. She felt...

She wasn't asking how she was feeling. She just was.

'I've had an inordinate amount of trouble,' he said.

'If you want me to say sorry, I'm not,' she whispered, and his hands stilled.

'I'll never ask you to say sorry,' he said. 'I'm the one...' His hands went back to massaging. They'd gentled a little. His massage was becoming almost an extension of his voice. 'Hell, Susie, if you hadn't been so lovely I'd never have found you. And I'd never have known that you needed to be found.'

'Wh—why?'

'When Effie remembered what she thought she might have

said to you, I was as close to murder as it's possible for a man to be and stay out of prison,' he said grimly. 'Of all the…' He paused, refocused, concentrating on small, concentric circles on either side of her spine. 'I was desperate to find you, but Donna told me I wasn't to come near you. I don't know what you wrote in your note to her, but she was feeling guilty as hell. The entire island's feeling guilty. They practically held me down.'

'So who's looking after the island medically now?' she demanded, feeling like she ought to ask something unemotional.

'Effie,' he said, and she blinked.

'Effie?'

'She's a doctor. In between being an astrologer.'

'Your Aunt Effie is a medical doctor?'

'Why do you think Grant and I ended up in the business? She used to read us medical journals as bedtime reading. By the time I was eight she was discussing cases, asking for opinions. She retired five years ago and has been driving me nuts ever since. But that's not what I'm here to talk about.'

'No?'

'No,' he said. 'Susie, this is a hell of a way to talk to you. I can't even see you.'

'You sent my masseur home,' she said. 'I believe I have another three quarters of an hour.'

'I don't…'

'Why are you here?' she asked. 'And don't stop whatever you're doing to my spine. If you knew how that feels…'

'I'm touching your skin, aren't I?' he demanded. 'I know how you're feeling.'

'You didn't to take me to bed.'

'I did.'

'Yeah, but you were too honourable. Because of Grant.'

'Not because of Grant.'

'Yes, because of Grant,' she snapped, and she would have

sat up, but then thought better of it and thumped herself down again. 'Massage.'

'Only because I wanted it to be different.'

'How could it be anything but different?'

'I've figured that out,' he said ruefully. 'Can I, please, stop massaging you now?'

'No.'

'I'm not being responsible,' he said.

'Good,' she said. 'Neither am I.'

'I've booked a honeymoon suite here,' he said, and she gasped.

'You've what?'

'Only until the morning. Then there's a yacht waiting for us in the Whitsundays.'

She thought about that for a moment, cautious. 'What sort of yacht?' she asked at last.

'A pink one.'

'A pink yacht.'

'It's called *Fluff and Nonsense*. It's the most irresponsible yacht I could find. It's got his and hers spa baths.'

'That's…'

'Ridiculous,' he told her. 'Totally irresponsible. All that water when one would do nicely. Save water. Bath with friends.'

'I can't…'

'Bath with friends? What about with a lover?'

'I…'

'By the way, I picked up your engagement ring,' he said. 'That was a very responsible thing you did, putting it in a bank vault. I had a jeweller reset it as a pendant. It cost me an arm and a leg, double because it was a rush job, but it's gorgeous,' He stopped massaging for a moment, fished in his pocket and draped a sliver of golden chain over her head. She gasped and caught it in her hand, The chain was just long enough for her to see—a perfect diamond set in a nest of rough gold. It was the most perfect thing she'd ever seen.

'Giving you this when I intend to give you another ring is probably not very sensible,' Sam said, sounding anxious. 'Irresponsible, would you say?'

'Irredeemable,' she managed.

'Excellent,' he said. 'Would you like to hear what other irresponsible things I've done?'

'I might.'

'I quit my job in the US without even having a contract to work here yet.'

'You know you can get a job here. That's not very irresponsible.'

'I've bought two Labrador puppies. And I've left Effie and Joel and Robbie and Brenda without so much as a can of dog food between them.'

'But I can't…'

'See, there's you being responsible,' he told her. 'You figure if anyone else isn't responsible then you have to pick up the pieces. I've left the breeder full details of the pups. They're going to check on them in a month and if the boys aren't looking after them to their satisfaction—and Joylene and Norris, Labrador breeders extraordinaire, are really particular in the way they want their puppies looked after—the pups will be taken back.'

'You can't…'

'I did. And I closed your pilates clinic until further notice.'

She sat up then. She sat bolt upright, swung round to face him, gasped as she remembered her lack of clothing, tugged her towel close and glared.

'You can't do that.'

'I did. I'm a very irresponsible person. Oh, I did sort of organise a water taxi to take people over to the mainland for the next two months. I did sort of find an exercise physiologist who's willing to take your equipment and run classes for a small fee. I did sort of happen to pay that fee.'

'Because you're responsible,' she whispered, but any anger she was feeling was fast turning into something else. He was looking at her with such a look…Tenderness. Desire. Love. All three, rolled into one. How could she ever have doubted it?

'I'll try really hard not to be,' he said humbly. 'I'll do whatever it takes. Because I love you, Susie. Yeah, I worried about Grant. Yeah, I thought I needed to show you I wasn't like him. But, hell, Susie, that you would possibly think I'd love you because of Grant…I love you despite Grant. No, that sounds wrong, too. I just plain love you. I love you, Susie, with all my heart, and I don't know how else I can say it. If it's pink yachts I'll do it. If it's diamonds I'll do it. If it's massaging you for ever…'

'That might work,' she whispered, blinking back tears.

'You've got it,' he said, and he cupped her face with his lovely hands and looked down into her eyes. 'Susie, you're not to cry.'

'I'm not crying.'

'You are crying. Oh, and I let the twins eat a half a dozen doughnuts after dinner on Thursday,' he said, remembering something obviously very important. 'Joel threw up on Brenda's knitting.'

'How…how horrible.'

'It was horrible. Even though Brenda's knitting turned out to be a potential scarf for me and it was even more horrible. You see,' he said tenderly. 'Whatever it takes.'

She choked on something between laughter and a sob. 'It doesn't take much,' she managed.

'Name it.'

'Just you,' she whispered. And then… 'Sam?'

'Mmm?'

'Maybe you'd better lock the door,' she said. 'Exercise physiologist making love to her orthopaedic surgeon in the massage room of an exclusive spa resort? How irresponsible is that?'

CHAPTER FOURTEEN

IT WAS a memorable day in the life of Ocean Spray.

First there was the official opening of the new bridge. There were politicians, dignitaries from all over, men and women in suits trying to give the impression that they'd made it happen, that politics was at work here, that the council was doing its job.

Everyone was quite happy to let them have their say. They'd helped, of course.

But it was Carly Hammond who cut the ribbon to the bridge on the mainland side. It was Pete Hammond, still with his arm in a sling but otherwise miraculously whole, who cut the ribbon in the other direction. And then the entire population of Ocean Spray walked from the island to the mainland and then walked back.

Of course, with an aging population there were people who couldn't manage the whole thing on foot. They were catered for with wheelchairs, but for such a demographic there were remarkably few. Maybe that was related to the vast banner fluttering over the bridge—WALK MADE POSSIBLE BY SUSIE'S EXERCISE REHABILITATION CENTRE, the sign said, even though Susie herself hadn't contributed monetarily. But the islanders had put the sign up and ignored her protests.

When they were all back on the island it was time for Pete's technology display. His system was designed to sense fog or darkness. Lights flickered across the bridge, flashing in vivid reds, picturesque even in daylight. At night they'd be spectacular.

In really thick fog an intermittent horn sounded, like a ship's fog horn, sounding mournfully out over the bay.

'And I promise never to skipper a boat again,' Pete said, to general laughter, and the occasion was over and it was time to move on to the next ceremony.

Which was even more important in the life of this island. For it was the wedding of Dr Sam Renaldo to the island's beloved Susie.

There were too many people to fit into the island's tiny church, so the ceremony was held on the beach just down from Susie's house.

It might get a bit busy here as the bridge carried traffic, Sam thought as he waited for his bride. They might be forced to move a little further round the island. But he'd already checked out land on a certain gorgeous cove. He hadn't told Susie yet, but the deeds were in their honeymoon baggage.

Maybe that was irresponsible.

She wouldn't care.

Susie had watched the bridge opening and then had disappeared to change. Sam waited for her on the beach, standing on the sand, feeling the sun on his face, knowing he was surrounded by friends, knowing he'd found his place on earth.

For today the bridge was closed to anyone but pedestrians. This was their last day of isolation. Pete and Carly were staying in Doris's spare room, but they were already thinking that they'd be the first of the incomers. There was a caveat on the island preventing development but there was room for a chosen few.

And this was the best place on earth.

They were all here. All these people that Sam had learned to love. This was his island.

Effie was being 'best man'. She was standing beside him,

beaming, looking important. Effie was their newest islander. She'd already opened a little family medical clinic, horoscopes given on the side.

The twins were turning cartwheels on the sand, waiting for their mother. They were dressed in hired suits, suits they'd chosen as being suitable. Suits that threatened to split before the bride arrived, but they didn't care. They were supposed to be ready to hold Susie's train, and they'd be responsible when the time came, but for now…their puppies were tumbling with them. Responsibility was for the future.

As it was for him, Sam thought. Responsibility came naturally with loving, but it didn't seem like responsibility. It just seemed like an extension of that love.

He loved Susie with all his heart.

And here she came. She was wearing the full bridal ensemble. 'You have to, Mum,' the boys had told her, and she'd grinned and agreed.

'Anything for a quiet life.'

But she'd loved the planning. Sam had listened with quiet satisfaction to her tales of days spent with Donna and Brenda and Effie, choosing a wedding gown, trying out wedding cakes, having hen nights, having fun.

This was the start of the rest of her life. She stood on the veranda steps, waiting for her boys to whoop up to her and take her train, and she smiled down at him and he thought his heart might break.

Susie.

Brenda was walking before her, tossing petals with gay abandon. Brenda in a truly awesome creation of pink chiffon and blue ribbons. Brenda for the first time in the history of the island without curlers.

Brenda in a hat that enveloped her head and stretched out almost to arm's length on either side.

And Susie.

She was exquisite. Yes, this was the full bridal ensemble, a white gown, a veil, a train. But she'd opted for simplicity and pure loveliness. Her scooped, sweetheart neckline and cinched waist showed her figure to perfection. The raw silk shimmered and shone in the morning sunlight. Her veil seemed to add to her loveliness, and when she walked down the beach to him, when Brenda giggled and helped lift her veil back, her loveliness took his breath away.

'That's the lot, Doc,' Brenda said, still giggling. 'You want to marry her now?'

'I intend to marry her,' Sam said, smiling deep into Susie's eyes. 'And Susie…do you intend to marry me?'

'Of course I do,' the bride whispered without a moment's hesitation. 'Let's get on with it. Haven't we booked the pink boat again for our honeymoon? Irresponsibility and happiness, here we come.'

Medical Romance™

COMING NEXT MONTH
TO MEDICAL ROMANCE SUBSCRIBERS

Visit www.eHarlequin.com for more details.

A PROPOSAL WORTH WAITING FOR by Lilian Darcy
Crocodile Creek 24-Hour Rescue
Surgeon Nick Devlin knows he's neglected his son, but going with him to Crocodile Creek Kids' Camp will change that. Nick is the last person Miranda expects to see there—their one passionate night at medical school left her with heartache, and she's determined to keep her distance....

THE SPANISH DOCTOR'S LOVE-CHILD by Kate Hardy
Mediterranean Doctors
Career-driven doctor Leandro Herrera never becomes emotionally involved with women. But then he discovers his new nurse is Becky Marston—the woman he spent one passionate night with.... And Becky announces she's pregnant! Suddenly the hot-blooded Spanish doctor wants the mother of his child as his wife!

A DOCTOR, A NURSE: A LITTLE MIRACLE by Carol Marinelli
Nurse Molly Jones has discovered that pediatrician Luke Williams is back—with four-year-old twins! Single dad Luke is charming—but Molly's heart was broken when Luke left, and when she discovered that, for her, motherhood was never meant to be.

TOP-NOTCH SURGEON, PREGNANT NURSE by Amy Andrews
Nursing manager Beth Rogers forgot her past for one amazing night, not expecting to see her English lover again. He turns out to be hotshot surgeon Gabe Fallon—and they'll be working together to save two tiny girls! Then Beth discovers she's carrying his baby.

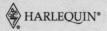

Inside ROMANCE

Stay up-to-date on all your romance reading news!

The Inside Romance newsletter is a FREE quarterly newsletter highlighting our upcoming series releases and promotions!

Click on the <u>Inside Romance</u> link on the front page of **www.eHarlequin.com** or e-mail us at insideromance@harlequin.ca to sign up to receive your FREE newsletter today!

You can also subscribe by writing us at: HARLEQUIN BOOKS Attention: Customer Service Department P.O. Box 9057, Buffalo, NY 14269-9057

Please allow 4-6 weeks for delivery of the first issue by mail.

IRN-IBPA208

Thoroughbred Legacy

The purse is set and the stakes are high…

Romance, scandal and glamour set in the exhilarating world of horse racing!

Follow the 12-book continuity, in September with:

Millions to Spare
by BARBARA DUNLOP
Book #5

Courting Disaster
by KATHLEEN O'REILLY
Book #6

Who's Cheatin' Who?
by MAGGIE PRICE
Book #7

A Lady's Luck
by KEN CASPER
Book #8

Available wherever books are sold, including most bookstores, supermarkets, discount stores and drugstores.